The Science
of Mental Health

The Editors of *Scientific American*

SCIENTIFIC | EDUCATIONAL
AMERICAN | PUBLISHING

New York

Published in 2025 by Scientific American Educational Publishing
in association with **The Rosen Publishing Group**
2544 Clinton Street, Buffalo NY 14224

Contains material from Scientific American®, a division of Springer Nature America, Inc.,
reprinted by permission, as well as original material from The Rosen Publishing Group®.

First Edition

Scientific American
Lisa Pallatroni: Project Editor

Rosen Publishing
Erica Grove: Compiling Editor
Michael Moy: Senior Graphic Designer

Cataloging-in-Publication Data
Names: Scientific American, Inc.
Title: The science of mental health / edited by the Scientific American Editors.
Description: First Edition. | New York : Scientific American Educational Publishing, 2025. |
Series: Scientific American explores big ideas | Includes bibliographical references and index.
Identifiers: ISBN 9781725351745 (pbk.) | ISBN 9781725351752
(library bound) | ISBN 9781725351769 (ebook)
Subjects: LCSH: Mental health–Juvenile literature. | Mental illness–Juvenile literature.
Classification: LCC RA790.S356 2025 | DDC 362.2–dc23

Manufactured in the United States of America
Websites listed were live at the time of publication.

Cover: GrAl/Shutterstock.com

CPSIA Compliance Information: Batch # CSSA25.
For Further Information contact Rosen Publishing at 1-800-237-9932.

CONTENTS

INTRODUCTION

To be mentally healthy is to have a sense of psychological, emotional, and social wellbeing. It helps enable us to handle stress and other challenging situations, get along well with others, and take care of ourselves. It also has a strong relationship to physical health, as mental illness contributes to a number of serious health conditions, including heart disease, diabetes, and strokes. The reasons why mental health should be a priority are plentiful, but there are many obstacles that can stand in the way of it.

According to the Centers for Disease Control and Prevention (CDC), over one in five American adults and youth ages 13 to 18 live with a mental illness, though the actual figures could be considerably larger, as mental illness often goes underreported. Among the more common mental illnesses are anxiety disorders, depression, eating disorders, post-traumatic stress disorder (PTSD), bipolar disorder, obsessive-compulsive disorder (OCD), and schizophrenia. These conditions can be debilitating and unfortunately are often stigmatized by society. However, there has been increased interest in gaining a better understanding of mental health and mental illness over the past few decades. This volume explores the entwined topics of mental health and mental illness from various angles.

Section 1, "Obstacles to Mental Health," examines some of the main challenges to mental health that people face today. These include mass shootings, climate change, the COVID pandemic, and relatively new technologies like social media, smartphones, and AI. Section 2, "The Science of Mental Illness," looks at scientific research that has facilitated greater understanding of the causes and impacts of mental illness. Section 3, "Habits for a Healthy Mind," offers information about lifestyle choices and other factors that can help promote mental health. Finally, Section 4—"Advancements in Mental Health Research and Treatment"—explains recent strides in mental health research that can help people living with mental illness experience less stigma and find a path to mental health.

Section 1: Obstacles to Mental Health

Is Too Little Play Hurting Our Kids?

By Joseph Polidoro

A long-term decline in unsupervised activity may be contributing to mental health declines in children and adolescents.

Peter Gray: It's not just moderate evidence. It's overwhelming evidence that if you take away children's opportunities for independent activity, they're not going to learn how to be independent, and that's going to lead them to be anxious and depressed, fearful about the future and all the things that we're seeing now.

Joseph Polidoro: It's been declared a national emergency. Mental health among children and adolescents decreased steadily between 2010 and 2020. By 2019, death by suicide had become the second-leading cause of death for those between age 10 and 24.

But this mental health decline may have been decades in the making. And according to a team of researchers, it's partly because we're not giving kids the independence they need.

For *Science, Quickly*, I'm Joseph Polidoro.

[CLIP: Music]

Gray: I'm Peter Gray. I'm a research professor of psychology and neuroscience at Boston College.

Polidoro: In the September issue of the *Journal of Pediatrics*, Gray and his co-authors observed a continuous increase in depression, anxiety, and suicide rates among children and adolescents since at least 1960. And they link it to a decline in unsupervised play and other independent activities.

Gray: Play is how children pursue what's fun for them. That's an immediate source of mental health—part of mental health really means "I'm happy" or "I'm most satisfied with my life right now."

Polidoro: Gray says that play and other independent activities also have far-reaching long-term effects on children's mental health and resilience.

Gray: I think that the real crisis is that young people are losing a sense of, "I can solve problems, I can deal with bumps in the road of life." And the way the children learn to do these things is through play where they are responsible to solve their own problems. They negotiate with their peers. They figure out how to solve quarrels among themselves. If somebody gets hurt, they figure out what to do about being hurt.

Polidoro: When kids are allowed to make decisions and solve problems, they exercise what's called their internal locus of control. They begin to feel they have control over experiences and their lives, rather than experiences controlling them.

Gray and his team cite work by psychologist Jean Twenge. She observed a dramatic increase in anxiety and depression from the 1960s through the 1990s. During the same timeframe, say Gray and his team, Twenge also reported a steep decline in internal locus of control. Gray says this correlation likely suggests that the decline in internal locus of control helps explain the mental health decline.

Gray: There's evidence for people of all ages that having a weak internal locus of control is predictive of future anxiety and depression. If you believe that anything can happen at any time and you can't do anything about it, that's a pretty anxiety-provoking view of life.

Polidoro: Control is also central to another set of established research, called self-determination theory. This research shows that children and adults have three basic psychological needs. If they're not fulfilled, we're not happy.

Gray: The first of those needs is autonomy. The sense that we have some freedom to choose what we're going to do, that we're in charge of our own life.

The second of these needs is competence. Not only am I free to choose what I want to do, but I can do it.

And the third is relatedness. It's also important that I have other people on my side on this. Connection with peers by this theory is an extremely important contributor to the sense of well-being.

Polidoro: These ideas are borne out in indigenous cultures, where very young children are close to their mothers until about the age of four. From that point on...

Gray: They are free to run and roam with other kids. They may be sent on errands. In every one of these cultures as far as have been studied, children have an enormous amount of freedom and also an enormous amount of responsibility. There's higher expectations of what children can do.

Polidoro: These anthropological findings suggest that from an evolutionary perspective, independent activity, personal responsibility, and self-initiated exploration and learning ideally begin at an early age.

It's a very convincing case, especially for anyone who remembers adolescents with paper routes, grade-school kids walking to school unsupervised, and kids of all ages playing together outside. But is the data there?

As Gray and his co-authors make very clear, they're presenting correlational evidence, albeit from many, many sources. And relying on correlations makes some scientists uneasy.

Cory Keyes: My name is Corey Keyes. I'm a professor of sociology, and I spent my career at Emory University.

Polidoro: Keyes does believe there's a case for play as a developmentally rich activity for kids.

Keyes: I think that's unequivocal in the research literature.

Polidoro: But...

Keyes: There's so many other things that have changed that would make me suspect that decline in play isn't just another sign of the mental health problem rather than a cause of it.

Polidoro: Stephan Collishaw also likes the argument but hesitates at its conclusions.

Stephan Collishaw: I'm a professor in developmental psychopathology at Cardiff University and also the co-director of the Wolfson Center for Young Peoples' Mental Health.

We need to be cautious about drawing a causal connection between those trends. And it's particularly, in my view, unclear how far we can kind of correlate broad social trends in aspects such as independent play and mental health.

Polidoro: Collishaw sees many changes over time that could be involved—school pressures, highly structured schedules, the mental health of parents, and the rise of digital technology.

Collishaw: It's hard to disentangle those and make a strong case that one has a causal effect on the other.

Polidoro: Still others who've looked closely at the data believe we can point to a reason more kids are more anxious and depressed than at any time in history.

Twenge: I've been doing work on generational differences for 30 years, and I got used to seeing changes that were big, but they would roll out slowly. And these changes in mental health were like nothing I'd ever seen. They were very, very sudden and very, very large.

My name is Jean Twenge. I am the author of the book *Generations*, the book *Igen*, and I'm a professor of psychology at San Diego State University.

Polidoro: Twenge sees another story in the data—a leveling off in mental health declines starting in the 1990s, and a huge increase 15 years later. And that rise coincided with—the smartphone.

Twenge: So we see these increases in depression starting in the early 2010s. That happens to be the same time when the majority of Americans first owned a smartphone. It's when social media use among teens moved from something that was optional, that about half of teens did every day, to something almost all of them— 75 percent, 80 percent—did every day.

Polidoro: Social media also became more visual around this time, Twenge says, as smartphones with front-facing cameras were introduced. Teens spent less time together and less time sleeping.

Twenge: So if you put these three things together—more time online, less time with friends face-to-face, less time sleeping—that's a very bad recipe for mental health.

Polidoro: Looking at the data, Twenge saw more than a time sequence lining up, but a huge and fundamental change to how teens spent their day-to-day lives—on-screen—just as teen depression started rising again. She could also rule out other possibilities.

Twenge: Economics are actually improving over that time. The unemployment rate was going down, the U.S. economy was finally starting to improve after the Great Recession.

We also know from several recent studies that these increases in anxiety and loneliness among teens are worldwide. That helps us rule out a lot of U.S.-based explanations around politics or school shootings or any of these other things because we see very, very similar patterns in other countries around the world.

Polidoro: Gray and his co-authors argue that there is little evidence that digital technology, including social media, can be linked to mental health declines—and that simply walling off social media, for instance, is just removing another opportunity for independence.

Twenge disagrees.

Twenge: That's just not correct. Social media is not just an individual issue. Social media is social. It has an impact at the level of the group.

Take a kid who doesn't have social media. Are they going to be able to live like it's 1988 and go out with their friends? No. Who are they going to go out with—because everybody else is on TikTok or Instagram at home. The whole social norm changed. These are group-level effects.

Polidoro: In fact, says Twenge, the case against social media—at least for teenage girls—may be stronger than the case against lead paint.

Twenge: In one of the best data sets that we've got, the correlation between hours of social media use a day and symptoms of depression among teen girls is 0.2. The correlation between childhood lead exposure and adult IQ is 0.11—about half the size. So again, I think that really makes that case that there are not small effects.

Polidoro: Still, Twenge thinks the data probably already exists for the kind of strong case for independent activity made in this paper.

Twenge: You have to take a broader view, or a more comprehensive view of the literature that's out there. You'd have to frame the argument differently for it to line up with the time sequence and acknowledge some of the tradeoffs involved.

Most public health experts would say that it's good that not as many high school students are drinking alcohol and having sex. Those independent activities trends are not all bad. There's trade-offs involved in them—they're not all good either.

Polidoro: So what should we make of all this?

Since there seem to be several factors in this mental health decline, as all of these researchers agree, there may be a number of necessary interventions. Still, Twenge thinks the data probably already exists for the kind of strong case for independent activity made in this paper.

Twenge: You have to take a broader view, or a more comprehensive view of the literature that's out there. You'd have to frame the argument differently for it to line up with the time sequence and acknowledge some of the tradeoffs involved.

Most public health experts would say that it's good that not as many high school students are drinking alcohol and having sex. Those independent activities trends are not all bad. There's trade-offs involved in them—they're not all good either.

Polidoro: Is that practical?

Twenge: We enforce age limits for driving. We enforce age limits for voting. We enforce age limits for alcohol. Why not do it for social media?

Polidoro: We also might change the way we think about mental health, says Keyes.

Keyes: This idea that the absence of mental illness is sufficient to describe somebody as "mentally healthy" is completely wrong. Mental health is more than the absence of mental illness. It's just that we are such a reactive society. We tend to think there's nothing wrong until somebody breaks down in terms of a medical category and that's simply not true.

Right now, I can tell you even among U.S. college students, it's an appalling rate of 30 percent to 40 percent of college students who aren't mentally ill, but they're not flourishing. They're in that middle category "languishing." And that's our college students.

Polidoro: Keyes would focus on improving the conditions for creating secure attachments in childhood.

Keyes: That meta-analysis about secure attachment showed that the greatest decline and the reason for the rise in insecurity is negative views of other people. The loss of trust and the inability to count on or depend on others to give you warm, trusting connection—and I think that's happening not because parents don't care, it's that they don't have enough time and encouragement and support and spending that kind of quality time to make those connections.

Polidoro: Gray agrees that the answer is more than just increased play. It's about giving children under 18 all the opportunities we can for independence, choice, interaction with peers, and individual growth.

Gray: It's not just play. It's an overall change in our view of young people's role in society and of young people's capacities. We're increasingly believing that young people are incompetent and can't be trusted to do things responsibly, and it becomes a self-fulfilling prophecy because we don't allow them those opportunities, they don't develop those opportunities.

[CLIP: Music]

Polidoro: *Science, Quickly* is produced by Jeffery DelViscio, Tulika Bose, Kelso Harper and Carin Leong. Our theme music was composed by Dominic Smith.

Like and subscribe wherever you get your podcasts. And for more in-depth science news and features, go to ScientificAmerican.com.

For *Scientific American's Science, Quickly,* I'm Joseph Polidoro.

Treating Mental Health as Part of Climate Disaster Recovery

By Anna Mattson

The U.S. has had an unprecedented year of climate disasters—a relentless whirlwind of droughts, floods, cyclones, and wildfires costing billions of dollars. Catastrophic events such as the firestorm in Hawaii and Hurricane Idalia in Florida have been battering down the homes and livelihoods of countless people, leaving trails of long-lasting destruction across the country.

Marty Dwyer, a disaster mental health supervisor with the American Red Cross, says the psychological impact of such sudden and massive losses can make it especially difficult to make big decisions in the aftermath, when they are often most urgently needed. And a hugely consequential choice immediately faces most survivors when they return to their destroyed homes: Should they stay and rebuild or migrate to someplace that seems safer?

"Whether you are a person experiencing homelessness or transiently unhoused because of disaster, that is a risk [to mental health]," says Joshua Morganstein, chair of the American Psychiatric Association's Committee on the Psychiatric Dimensions of Disaster. Morganstein has worked with survivors of mass shootings, Hurricane Katrina, and various wildfires, and has witnessed firsthand how disaster trauma impacts mental wellbeing.

A growing body of research is revealing how crises of climate change—including wildfire smoke, pollution, flooding, and extreme heat—are worsening conditions such as anxiety, depression, and post-traumatic stress disorder (PTSD). While experts emphasize the importance of quickly getting people rehoused, rebuilding in a disaster-prone area could subject people to the trauma of losing their home yet again.

Scientific American spoke with Morganstein and Dwyer about the correlation between housing and mental health post-disaster and about measures to prevent repeated traumatization as these disasters persist.

[An edited transcript of the interview follows.]

SCIENTIFIC AMERICAN: How does climate disaster trauma differ from other kinds and symptoms of trauma?

DWYER: A climate disaster raises the level of trauma significantly when people don't have a chance to prepare and wait. For example, with the wildfire in Maui, they basically had no notice. But in all disasters, you see some pretty similar responses: people might be feeling just absolutely overwhelmed or numb or experiencing high levels of anxiety. It's not uncommon for people to be very angry.

The first things I see are more physical complaints. People describe having insomnia, diminished appetite, headaches, or stomachaches. On top of that, many people have preexisting mental health conditions or they have had prior trauma that makes them more likely to need additional assistance.

MORGANSTEIN: People who are exposed to any given disaster have different types of exposure. Many people experience distress, annoyances, and general stressors. And there can be many of those that pile up on top of one another. Of course, the stresses that people experience change over time. The stresses of the moment of a hurricane are very different from the stress of two weeks, six weeks, six months, and 12 months after the event.

Immediate stress reactions include feeling unsafe, which causes significant negative health effects. People who feel unsafe, for instance, are more likely to have difficulty with sleep, and they're more likely to increase their use of alcohol and tobacco. They're also more likely to indicate symptoms of general distress.

Some people may ultimately develop psychiatric disorders. Most often we think about PTSD in the event of a disaster. PTSD is not the most frequent disorder, however. Depression is more common.

It's hard enough to move to a new place when you *want* to, and you've planned for it, and all of your possessions are with you. But people who have been forcefully displaced are dealing with issues of grief, which is a very overlooked but universal response to disasters. It's often the thing that hangs on for people long after scars are healed. Mental health professionals will diagnose depression, anxiety, or PTSD. But we as a society do not do a very good job, I think, at anticipating and addressing the almost universal issue of grief that happens in the wake of all disaster events.

SA: Why is housing important to mental health in post-disaster relief?

MORGANSTEIN: There are negative physical health and mental health effects that become enhanced when people are unhoused.

Many people who are displaced find themselves in shelters, makeshift or otherwise, with a bunch of strangers. They are without comfort or things that make them feel safe—such as a locked door or just some place to go where they don't feel exposed to other people. People have difficulty sleeping in loud, noisy places, and they're limited in their ability to protect whatever property they're able to take. When someone has chronically underslept, almost everything in their life gets worse: their ability to make decisions, to exercise good judgment, to take protective actions, to assess threats properly in ways that protect themselves and their family.

In an attempt to address that, hotels have offered support and have tried to be good stewards in their community after disasters. They move people into their facilities. Being in a place where your family can go and be together and lock a door will help some people to feel safer. People find they can connect with, learn from, or share adversity with others who are going through this difficult situation. But one of the things that this might also do is lead some people to feel isolated. Different people have different needs.

DWYER: Housing is very, very important. One of the things we have seen, especially during the COVID pandemic, is that organizations in the U.S. seem to be getting people out of congregate group shelters and moving towards what we refer to as "noncongregate shelters" [such as hotels]. It might not be home, but it's not a large building where you're sleeping right next to strangers.

SA: What are some pros and cons of staying and rebuilding?

MORGANSTEIN: Some people leave because they feel a sense of threat and feel unsafe. Disasters often do not just take people out of their home but also scatter the community. Everyone disperses because their communities were wiped out by a tornado, hurricane, or wildfire. Everyone had to move. Now all of that support is sort of gone. It's probably important to think about the extent to which people choose to stay versus people who simply do not have the means or resources to go [who say] "I'm here because I have no other choice."

For others, staying can be a way to build a sense of resilience. It can be a path to recovery to go back to and to be present in a place where something difficult happened. We have to remember that most people, even people who have difficulties along the way, will ultimately be OK—and this is very important. Eventually people are able to make meaning of those events. And at some point, people can look hopefully to the future.

SA: How can people rebuilding in disaster-sensitive areas prevent retraumatization?

MORGANSTEIN: The fundamental framework for interventions that we know protect mental health, foster resilience, and improve people's ability to function after disasters involves five essential elements: enhancing a sense of safety, calming, social connectedness, self- or community efficacy, and hope. Before it gets to the point where we're talking about medications and therapies, fostering those five essential elements really is the framework for protecting people who are experiencing extreme stress.

We also want to remind people of their innate strengths and capabilities. When we see someone doing something, our goal is not to take over and do everything for a person. We might feel, "Oh, my gosh, this person has been through so much. I'm just going to help them." Unfortunately, when we do everything for someone, the feeling of helplessness can almost be exacerbated. Helping someone to know where to go encourages them to take those steps. Lower those barriers for people who are having a lot of difficulties.

Is it going to be worse or better? I'd like to be able to give you a simple answer to whether people should come back. The reality is that there are many factors for individuals that will likely come into play. I do think it's important to think about—because these events are happening more frequently.

If you simply search the literature for "repeat disasters," there isn't a lot out there to show what happens over time for people who are exposed to events over and over again. Certainly we have some evidence to show that after difficult situations, people learn from them and feel better equipped to handle them in the future.

DWYER: Our goal is not to replace the community resources. We are there to supplement and strengthen what the local community has in place, especially in places such as Hawaii or Puerto Rico, where the culture is so important. We want people to get support in a culturally sensitive way. We come from all over; we don't necessarily know what it's like to live in that community.

If you can alleviate immediate emotional distress, it really does make a difference. Most individuals and families are able to function adequately after a disaster. They may not be as effective in their daily activities. They may have difficulty processing and problem solving, for example. But most people, as devastating as [the disaster] seems, are able to move forward. We help them to discover their resilience and take those first steps.

About the Author

Anna Mattson is a freelance science journalist based in South Dakota. You can find more of her work at annamattson.com or follow her on X (formerly Twitter) @AnnaMattson9.

'AI Anxiety' Is on the Rise— Here's How to Manage It

By Lauren Leffer

It's logical for humans to feel anxious about artificial intelligence. After all, the news is constantly reeling off job after job at which the technology seems to outperform us. But humans aren't yet headed for all-out replacement. And if you do suffer from so-called AI anxiety, there are ways to alleviate your fears and even reframe them into a motivating force for good.

In one recent example of generative AI's achievements, AI programs outscored the average human in tasks requiring originality, as judged by human reviewers. For a study published this month in *Scientific Reports*, researchers gave 256 online participants 30 seconds to come up with imaginative uses for four commonplace objects: a box, a rope, a pencil, and a candle. For example, a box might serve as a cat playhouse, a miniature theater, or a time capsule. The researchers then gave the same task to three different large language models. To assess the creativity of these responses, the team used two methods: an automated program that assessed "semantic distance," or relatedness between words and concepts, and six human reviewers that were trained to rank responses on their originality.

In both assessments, the highest-rated human ideas edged out the best of the AI responses—but the middle ground told a different story. The mean AI scores were significantly higher than the mean human scores. For instance, both the automated and human assessments ranked the response "cat playhouse" as less creative than a similar AI-generated response from GPT-4, "cat amusement park." And people graded the lowest-scoring human answers as far less creative than the worst of the AI generations.

Headlines ensued, proclaiming that "AI chatbots already surpass average human in creativity" and "AI is already more creative than YOU." The new study is the latest in a growing body of research that seems to portend generative AI outpacing the average human in many artistic and analytical realms—from photography competitions to scientific hypotheses.

It's news such as this that has fed Kat Lyons's fears about AI. Lyons is a Los Angeles–based background artist who works in animation and creates immersive settings for TV shows including *Futurama* and *Disenchantment*. In many ways, it's their dream job—a paid outlet for their passion and skill in visual art, which they've been cultivating since age four. But some aspects of the dream have begun to sour: the rise of visual generative AI tools such as Midjourney and Stable Diffusion (and the entertainment industry's eagerness to use them) has left Lyons discouraged, frustrated, and anxious about their future in animation—and about artistic work in general. For instance, they were disheartened when Marvel and Disney decided to use an AI-generated, animated intro sequence made by the visual effects company Method Studios for the show *Secret Invasion*, which premiered in June. "It feels really scary," Lyons says. "I honestly hate it." Disney, which owns Marvel Studios, and Method Studios did not immediately respond to a request for comment.

Like many professional creatives, Lyons now worries about AI models—which need to train themselves on vast swaths of internet content—stealing and rehashing their artistic work for others' profit. And then there's the corresponding loss of employment opportunities. More broadly, Lyons fears for the future of art itself in an era when honing a craft and a personal voice are no longer prerequisites for producing seemingly original and appealing projects. "I worked so hard for my artistic dreams. I've been drawing since I was in preschool," they say. "This is always what I've wanted to do, but we might be entering a world where I have to give that up as my full-time job—where I have to go back to waiting tables or serving coffee."

Lyons isn't alone. Many people have found themselves newly anxious about the rapid rise of generative AI, says Mary Alvord, a practicing psychologist in the Washington, D.C., area. Alvord says her clients of all ages express concerns about artificial intelligence.

22

Specific worries include a lack of protection for online data privacy, the prospect of job loss, the opportunity for students to cheat, and even the possibility of overall human obsolescence. AI's advance has triggered a vague but pervasive sense of general public unease, and for some individuals, it has become a significant source of stress.

As with any anxiety, it's important to manage the emotion and avoid becoming overwhelmed. "A certain amount of anxiety helps motivate, but then too much anxiety paralyzes," Alvord says. "There's a balance to strike." Here's how some psychologists and other experts suggest tackling our AI fears.

First off, context is key, says Sanae Okamoto, a psychologist and behavioral scientist at the United Nations University–Maastricht Economic and Social Research Institute on Innovation and Technology in the Netherlands. She suggests keeping in mind that the present moment is far from the first time people have feared the rise of an unfamiliar technology. "Computer anxiety" and "technostress" date back decades, Okamoto notes. Before that, there was rampant worry over industrial automation. Past technological advances have led to big societal and economic shifts. Some fears materialized, and some jobs did disappear, but many of the worst sci-fi predictions did not come true.

"It's natural and historical that we are afraid of any new technology," says Jerri Lynn Hogg, a media psychologist and former president of the American Psychological Association's Society for Media Psychology and Technology. But understanding the benefits of a new tech, learning how it works, and getting training in how to use it productively can help—and that means going beyond the headlines.

Simone Grassini, one of the researchers of the new study and a psychologist at Norway's University of Bergen, is quick to point out that "performing one specific task that is related to creative behavior doesn't automatically translate to 'AI can do creative jobs.' " The current technology is not truly producing new things but rather imitating or simulating what people can do, Grassini says. AI's "cognitive architecture and our cognitive architecture are substantially different." In the study, it's possible the AI won high creativity ratings because its answers simply copied verbatim parts of a human creation contained somewhere in its training set, he explains. The AI was also competing against human volunteers who had no particular motivation to excel at their creative task and had never necessarily completed such an assignment before. Participants were recruited online and paid only about $2.50 for an estimated 13 minutes of work.

Confronting fears of generative AI by actually trying out the tools, seeing where and how they can be useful, reading up on how they work, and understanding their limitations can turn the tech from a boogeyman into a potential asset, Hogg says. A deeper understanding can empower someone to advocate for meaningful job protections or policies that rein in potential downsides.

Alvord also emphasizes the importance of addressing the problem directly. "We talk about what actions you can take instead of sticking your head in the sand," she says. Maybe that means gaining new skills to prepare for a career change or learning about ongoing efforts to regulate AI. Or maybe it means building a coalition with colleagues at work. Lyons says being involved with their union, the Animation Guild, has been crucial to helping them feel more secure and hopeful about the future. In this way, remedies for AI anxiety may be akin to ones for another major, burgeoning societal fear: climate anxiety. Though there are obvious differences between the two phenomena (AI clearly offers some significant possible benefits), there are also apparent similarities. In tackling the biggest concerns about AI and in confronting the climate crisis, "we're all in this challenge together," Okamoto says. Just as with climate activism, she explains, meaningfully confronting fears over AI might begin with building solidarity, finding community, and coming up with collective solutions.

Another way to feel better about AI is to avoid overly fixating on it, Okamoto adds. There is more to life than algorithms and screens. Taking breaks from technology to reconnect with nature or loved ones in the physical world is critical for mental health, she notes. Stepping away from tech can also provide a reminder of all the ways that humans are distinct from the chatbots or image generators that might threaten a person's career or self-image. Humans, unlike AI, can experience the world directly and connect with one another about it.

When people create something, it's often in response to their environment. Each word or brushstroke can carry meaning. For Lyons, human creativity is a "feral, primitive drive to make something because you can't not make it." So far, all AI can do is mimic that ability and creative motivation, says Sean Kelly, a Harvard University philosophy professor who has been examining the relationship between human creativity and AI for years. When an AI model generates something, Kelly says, "it's not doing what the original artist did, which was trying to say something that they felt needed to be said."

To Kelly, the real societal fear shouldn't be that AI will get better or produce ever more interesting content. Instead he's afraid "that we'll give up on ourselves" and "just become satisfied" with what AI generators can provide.

Perhaps the better, and more characteristically human, response is to use our AI anxiety to propel us forward. Mastering a craft—be it drawing, writing, programming, translating, playing an instrument, or composing mathematical proofs—and using that skill to create something new is "the most rewarding thing that we can possibly do," Kelly says. So why not let AI motivate more creation instead of replace it? If the technology spits out something compelling, we can build on it. And if it doesn't, then why worry about it at all?

About the Author

Lauren Leffer is a contributing writer and former tech reporting fellow at Scientific American. *She reports on many subjects including artificial intelligence, climate, and weird biology because she's curious to a fault. When she's not writing, she's hopefully hiking. Follow her on X (formerly Twitter) @lauren_leffer and on Bluesky @laurenleffer.bsky.social.*

Why Just One Sleepless Night Makes People Emotionally Fragile

By Eti Ben Simon

When I was a graduate student, my colleagues and I studied how losing one night of sleep affects a person's ability to manage their emotions. Once a week, typically on a Friday evening, I would stay up all night to monitor our participants and ensure that they followed the protocol. At about noon the next day, we would all stumble out of the laboratory, exhausted and eager to get home and rest.

Two months into the experiment, I was in my car at a traffic light when a silly love song started playing on the radio. Suddenly, I was crying uncontrollably. I remember feeling surprised at my reaction. It then hit me that I was not just studying sleep deprivation—I had become *part* of the study. Weeks of missed sleep had taken their toll, and I was no longer in control of my emotions.

That research project, and many that have followed since, demonstrated a strong and intimate link between better sleep and emotional health. In healthy individuals, good-quality sleep is linked with a more positive mood—and it takes just one night of sleep deprivation to trigger a robust spike in anxiety and depression the following morning. Moreover, people who suffer from chronic sleep disruption tend to experience daily events as more negative, making it hard to escape a gloomy mindset. Indeed, in a national sleep survey, 85 percent of Americans reported mood disruption when they were not able to get enough sleep.

Studies from our lab and others are now beginning to illuminate just how a lack of sleep frays the inner fabric of our mind. One of its many impacts is to disrupt the brain's circuitry for regulating emotions.

For decades researchers and medical professionals considered sleep loss a by-product or symptom of another, more "primary" condition, such as depression or anxiety. In other words, *first* comes the anxiety, and then sleep loss follows. Today we know that this order can be reversed. In fact, sleep loss and anxiety, depression, or other mental health conditions may feed into one another, creating a downward spiral that is exceedingly difficult to break.

Much evidence in this area comes from chronic sleeplessness or insomnia. People who suffer from insomnia are at least twice as likely to develop depression or anxiety later in life, compared with individuals who sleep well. For instance, a study that followed 1,500 individuals—some with insomnia and others without—found that chronic sleeplessness was associated with a three times greater increase in the onset of depression a year later and twice the increase in the onset of anxiety.

Insomnia symptoms also raise the risk of developing post-traumatic stress disorder and track closely with suicidal behavior among at-risk individuals. They often precede a mood episode in people with bipolar disorder. Even after adequate treatment for depression or anxiety, people who continue to suffer from sleep difficulties are at greater risk of relapse relative to those whose sleep improves. Understanding sleep's role in this pattern could unlock insights for helping to prevent and treat many emotional and mental disorders.

Older research already revealed that sleep loss can precede serious mental health symptoms in otherwise healthy individuals. In studies conducted mostly in the 1960s, volunteers who stayed awake for more than two nights reported difficulties forming thoughts, finding words, and composing sentences. They suffered from hallucinations, such as seeing inanimate objects move or experiencing the sensation of another's touch despite being alone. After three days without sleep, some participants became delusional and paranoid. They believed they were secret agents or that aliens were contacting them. (If that sounds like a psychotic episode, that's because it is.) After five days, several participants entered a state resembling a full-blown clinical psychosis and were unable to fully comprehend their circumstances.

In one study from 1947, volunteers from the U.S. military attempted to stay awake for more than four nights. A soldier who was described by his friends as quiet and reserved became extremely aggressive after three nights without sleep. He provoked fights and insisted he was on a secret mission for the president. Eventually he was forcibly restrained and dismissed from the experiment. Six others exhibited outbursts of violence and persistent hallucinations. In all cases, after sleeping for an entire day, the soldiers behaved normally again and had no recollection of the earlier mayhem. In another study, in which participants stayed awake for four nights, researchers were unprepared for the "frequent psychotic features" they encountered, such as intense hallucinations and paranoid delusions.

Given these destructive effects, studies of prolonged sleep loss are now considered to be unethical, but they still offer a powerful reminder of just how sleep-dependent our minds and mental health truly are.

Even with these startling results, scientists have been skeptical about the consequences of restless nights, particularly given that (fortunately) few of us endure such extreme deprivation. That's where the newest wave of research comes in. In recent years a neuroscientific explanation has emerged that is beginning to illuminate what it is about sleep, or the lack of it, that seems to have a direct link to our emotions.

Whenever we face a nerve-wracking or emotionally intense challenge, a hub deep in the brain called the amygdala kicks into gear. The amygdala can trigger a comprehensive whole-body response to prepare us for the challenge or threat we face. This flight-or-fight response increases our heart rate and sends a wave of stress hormones rushing into our bloodstream. Luckily, there's one brain region standing between us and this cascade of hyperarousal: the prefrontal cortex, an area right behind the middle of our eyebrows. Studies show that activity in this region tends to dampen, or downregulate, the amygdala, thus keeping our emotional response under control.

In studies where my colleagues and I deprived healthy volunteers of one night of sleep, they discovered that the activity of the prefrontal cortex dropped drastically, as measured using functional magnetic resonance imaging (fMRI). Moreover, the neural activity linking the amygdala and the prefrontal cortex became significantly weaker. In other words, both the region and the circuit meant to keep our emotional reactions under control are essentially out of order when sleep is disrupted. Other studies have found that this profile of neural impairment can occur in people after they experience just one night of sleep deprivation, in people who are habitual short sleepers, or when participants' sleep is restricted to only four hours a night for five nights.

This impairment can be so robust that it blurs the lines around what people consider emotional. For example, when my colleagues and I exposed participants to neutral and emotional pictures (think bland images of commuters on a train versus photographs of children crying), fMRI revealed that the amygdala responded differently to these prompts when people were well rested. But after losing a night of sleep, a person's amygdala responded strongly to *both* kinds of images. In other words, the threshold for what the brain deems emotional became significantly lower when the amygdala could not act in concert with the prefrontal cortex. Such impaired emotional control makes us more vulnerable to anxiety and poor mood, so that even silly love songs can trigger sobbing.

The effects on the amygdala, the prefrontal cortex, and the circuitry between the two may have many other consequences as well. In January we published findings that show that changes in this brain circuit, together with other regions involved in arousal, relate to increases in blood pressure after one night of sleep loss. The brain-level mechanisms my colleagues and I have observed may contribute to changes that negatively affect the entire body, increasing the risk for hypertension and cardiovascular disease.

Stepping back, it becomes clear that—like our physical well-being—mental and emotional health rely on a delicate balance. Myriad choices we make throughout the day *and* night maintain that balance. Even a single sleepless night can therefore do damage. We need to be mindful of this reality, for both ourselves and one another. Inevitably we all miss out on sleep from time to time. But our societies should critically examine structures—such as work norms, school cultures, and the lack of support for parents or other caregivers—that prevent people from getting enough rest. The science of sleep and mental health suggests that failing to address those problems will leave people vulnerable to serious harm.

About the Author

Eti Ben Simon is a research scientist at the University of California, Berkeley. She studies the emotional and social consequences of sleep loss on the human brain and body.

How Much Worry about Mass Shootings Is Too Much?

By Stephanie Pappas

A shopping mall in Texas, a private school in Tennessee, a bank in Kentucky, and a dance studio in California: these are the sites of some of the public mass shootings in the U.S. in 2023 alone, representing just a slice of the presumed safe spaces rocked by these tragedies. As mass shootings in the country have risen, evidence is mounting that they are having a far-reaching mental health impact. A 2019 survey by the American Psychological Association (APA) found that 79 percent of Americans reported stress over the possibility of a mass shooting, and 33 percent said fear of a shooting prevented them from going to certain places.

Now new research published on May 23 in *Death Studies* finds that at the far end of this continuum are people whose anxiety about mass shootings has become dysfunctional, or almost a phobia. A few key symptoms—such as hypervigilance, changes in appetite, and dreams about mass killings—indicate someone might need mental health support, says the study's author Sherman Lee, a psychologist at Christopher Newport University in Virginia.

"I'm trying to find that line of how much worry is too much worry," says Lee, whose new research validates a mass shooting anxiety scale that could help screen people for this type of dysfunctional dread.

People have a broad range of responses to mass tragedies, says Roxane Cohen Silver, a psychologist at the University of California, Irvine, who studies the effects of collective trauma and was not involved in the new study. "There are certainly people who go about their day-to-day experiences without thinking about mass shootings at all," Silver says. Others, she says, change their behavior dramatically, avoiding certain public places or even homeschooling their children.

31

The fear could be exacerbated by the frequency of false alarms, says Rachel Rizvi, a business intelligence developer in Denver whose oldest child attends high school. Over the course of her child's freshman year in 2022 and 2023, Rizvi says the school went into full lockdown or closed the campus for security reasons seven times—triggering text messages and email alerts to parents.

"As soon as I get that email, my heart jumps into my throat," Rizvi says, "because there are no details. You have no idea if it's happening at your child's school [or] a school that's close by. You don't know if police are on site.... As a parent, you start thinking, 'Did I see my kid for the last time this morning?' Doing that for even an hour feels like forever."

Rizvi says the frequent lockdowns at her child's school are a factor in her family's decision to move to a smaller district, where she hopes smaller schools and more personal attention will reduce the danger. "I know it can happen anywhere," she says, "but I'm just hoping that maybe from a statistical standpoint, the odds are even slightly smaller."

In the APA survey, parents, in particular, were impacted. Twenty-eight percent of those with kids under the age of 18 reported frequent or constant stress about mass shootings, compared with 16 percent of people without minor children. Sixty-two percent of parents said they worried their child might become a victim. Black and Hispanic adults were also more likely than non-Hispanic white adults to express fears that they or someone they know would become a victim or to report stress over mass shootings.

There are no firm numbers on how many people experience so much stress that they lose the ability to function well in daily life—but there are hints that a subset of people struggle a lot. For instance, in a paper published this month in *JMIR Public Health and Surveillance*, researchers reported a spike in calls to a mental health crisis line after the 2022 shooting at an elementary school in Uvalde, Tex. There was also an accompanying increase in conversations about firearms and grief.

Lee's new work suggests that certain symptoms are associated with poor coping. His new screening questionnaire focuses on five symptoms to determine whether anxiety might be affecting a person's daily functioning. One symptom is appetite change when thinking about mass shooting, indicating high levels of stress and fear, Lee says. Another is a physical response such as sweating or a pounding heart when thinking about these events. Such symptoms indicate that a person's "fight-or-flight" response is kicking in, putting the body on high alert.

Dreaming about mass shootings and experiencing hypervigilance are two more signs that a person's mental processes are in "a mode of anxiety," Lee says. Finally, avoidant behavior—such as staying home for fear of a mass shooting—is another sign. Experiencing these symptoms for several days over a two-week period may indicate the need for mental health support, he says.

Fortunately there are highly effective treatments for anxiety, Lee says, including cognitive behavioral therapy delivered virtually. Another strategy for better coping might be to limit media exposure to information about mass shootings. In a 2019 paper published in *Science Advances*, Silver and her colleagues found that people who read or watched a lot of news about the Boston Marathon bombing in 2013 became more distressed, which in turn led them to consume more media during the Pulse nightclub shooting in Orlando, Fla., in 2016, leading to still more worry. The effects of this exposure seem to be cumulative.

"We don't see people becoming habituated," Silver says. "Instead we see that there is increased anxiety."

About the Author

Stephanie Pappas is a freelance science journalist. She is based in Denver, Colo.

Social Media Can Harm Kids. Could New Regulations Help?

By Jesse Greenspan

This week Surgeon General Vivek H. Murthy released a warning about the risks that social media presents to the mental health of children and teenagers. Adolescent mental health has been declining for years, and an increasing amount of research suggests that social media platforms could be partially to blame. But experts continue to debate just how much impact they have—and whether new and proposed laws will actually improve the situation or will end up infringing on free speech without addressing the root of the problem.

Numerous studies demonstrate that adolescent rates of depression, anxiety, loneliness, self-harm, and suicide have skyrocketed in the U.S. and elsewhere since around the time that smartphones and social media became ubiquitous. In fact, in the U.S., suicide is now the leading cause of death for people aged 13 to 14 and the second-leading cause of death for those aged 15 to 24. In October 2021 the American Academy of Pediatrics declared a "national state of emergency in children's mental health," stating that the COVID pandemic had intensified an already existing crisis. The U.S. Centers for Disease Control and Prevention issued a similar warning in 2022, after the agency found that nearly half of high school students reported feeling persistently "sad or hopeless" during the previous year. According to the CDC, LGBTQ and female teens appear to be suffering particularly poor mental health.

Yet the role social media plays has been widely debated. Some researchers, including Jean Twenge of San Diego State University and Jonathan Haidt of New York University, have sounded the alarm, arguing that social media provides the most plausible explanation for problems such as enhanced teen loneliness. Other researchers have been more muted. In 2019 Jeff Hancock, founding director of the Social Media Lab at Stanford University, and his colleagues completed a meta-analysis of 226 scientific papers dating back to 2006 (the year Facebook became available to the public). They concluded that social media use was associated with a slight increase in depression and anxiety but also commensurate improvements in feelings of belonging and connectedness.

"At that time, I thought of them as small effects that could balance each other out," Hancock says. Since then, however, additional studies have poured in—and he has grown a bit more concerned. Hancock still believes that, for most people most of the time, the effects of social media are minor. He says that sleep, diet, exercise. and social support, on the whole, impact psychological health more than social media use. Nevertheless, he notes, social media can be "psychologically very detrimental" when it's used in negative ways—for instance, to cyberstalk former romantic partners. "You see this with a lot of other addictive behaviors like gambling, for example," Hancock says. "Many people can gamble, and it's not a problem. But for a certain subset, it's really problematic."

Some recent studies have attempted to clarify the link between social media and mental health, asking, for instance, whether social media use is causing depression or whether people are being more active on social media because they're depressed. In an attempt to present causal evidence, Massachusetts Institute of Technology economist Alexey Makarin and two of his colleagues compared the staggered rollout of Facebook across various U.S. colleges from 2004 to 2006 with mental health surveys taken by students at that time. Their study, published in 2022, found that swollen rates of depression and anxiety, as well as diminished academic performance, followed Facebook's arrival. Makarin says much of the harm they documented came from social comparisons: students viewed the online profiles of their peers and believed them to "[have] nicer lives, party more often, have more friends and look better than them." Facebook's parent company Meta did not respond to requests for comment by press time.

Other studies have obtained similar results. In one paper, participants were paid to deactivate Facebook for four weeks prior to the 2018 U.S. midterm elections and reported experiencing improved happiness and life satisfaction when they weren't on the platform. And in February 2023 researchers at Swansea University in Wales found likely physical health benefits, including a boost to the functioning of the immune system, when social media use was reduced by as little as 15 minutes per day.

"In total, there's a more and more coherent picture that, indeed, social media has a negative impact on mental health," Makarin says. "We are not saying that social media can explain 100 percent of the rise of mental health issues.... But it could potentially explain a sizeable portion."

Mitch Prinstein, chief science officer at the American Psychological Association (APA), which recently released recommendations for adolescent social media use, points out that there's nothing inherently harmful or beneficial about social media. "If I'm 12, and I'm reading *Scientific American* and going on social media to talk with my friends about how interesting the articles are," he says, then that's a far cry from "going on a site that's showing me how to cut myself and hide it from my parents." He suggests that social media companies should take down the potentially harmful content, letting youth use social media more safely.

In addition to toxic content, Prinstein worries about the effects of social media on young people's sleep—and therefore brain development. "No kid should be on their phone after 9 p.m.," he says, "unless they're going to sleep well into the morning." But actually closing down the social apps and putting that phone down is difficult, Prinstein says. This is in part because of the design of these platforms, which aim to hold users' attention for as long as possible. Kris Perry, executive director of the nonprofit Children and Screens: Institute of Digital Media and Child Development and a former senior adviser to California governor Gavin Newsom, agrees. Besides being sucked in by app design, she says, adolescents fear disappointing their peers. "Kids feel genuinely scared that they'll lose friendships, that they won't be popular, if they don't like their friends' posts instantly," Perry says.

The flood of new studies on social media's harms is spurring lawmakers to action. Except for the Children's Online Privacy Protection Act, which passed in 1998—years prior to the advent of smartphones or social media—the U.S. Congress has never really involved itself with what kids do online. "It's kind of the Wild West out there," Prinstein says of the lack of oversight. Since around 2021, however, when a Facebook whistleblower testified that the company knew its platforms harmed youth mental health—allegations that Facebook denied—both Republican and Democratic lawmakers have moved to follow Europe's lead on stronger Internet regulations. On the federal level, members of Congress have introduced a slew of overlapping bills: at least two would bar social media use outright for kids under a certain age, while others would restrict targeted advertising and data collection, give young users more control over their personal information, prioritize parental supervision, facilitate additional research and hold social media companies liable for toxic content viewed by minors. Though nothing has yet passed, President Joe Biden seems largely onboard with these measures. In his February State of the Union speech, Biden said, "We must finally hold social media companies accountable for the experiment they are running on our children for profit." And on the same day as the surgeon general's warning this week, the White House commissioned a task force to analyze how to improve the health, safety, and privacy of kids who go online.

Meanwhile state legislatures have jumped into the fray. California recently passed a law designed to protect children's online data. Montana banned TikTok. And Arkansas and Utah mandated, among other things, that social media companies verify the ages of their users and that minors get parental consent to open an account. Similar bills are pending in many other states.

Of the federal bills currently pending, arguably the Kids Online Safety Act (KOSA) has gained the most attention thus far. Sponsored by Republican Senator Marsha Blackburn of Tennessee and Democratic Senator Richard Blumenthal of Connecticut, the bill would require social media companies to shield minors from content deemed dangerous. It also aims to safeguard personal information and rein in addictive product features such as endless scrolling and autoplaying. Supporters of KOSA include Children and Screens, the APA, and the American Academy of Pediatrics, along with several parents whose kids died by suicide after being relentlessly cyberbullied.

On the opposing side, organizations that include the Electronic Frontier Foundation, a digital rights nonprofit, and the American Civil Liberties Union have come out against KOSA, stating that it might increase online surveillance and censorship. For instance, these parties have raised concerns that state attorneys general could weaponize the act to suppress content about, say, transgender health care or abortion. This is particularly problematic because it could negate some of the positive effects social media has on teen mental health.

Researchers acknowledge that social media can aid kids by, among other things, connecting them with like-minded people and facilitating emotional support. This appears to be especially important for "folks from underrepresented backgrounds," Prinstein says, "whether you're the only person around who looks like you or the only person with your identity in your family." If KOSA leads to the restriction of speech about LGBTQ issues, for instance, it could be detrimental to members of that community. "That support, and even accessing information, is a great benefit," Prinstein says. "There really was no other way to get that resource in the olden times."

Jason Kelley, associate director of digital strategy at the Electronic Frontier Foundation, says that rather than a bill like KOSA, he would prefer to see stronger antitrust laws that might, for example, increase competition among platforms, which could encourage each one to improve its user experience in order to win out. More options, he says, would force social media companies "to deal with the ways they ignore user interest and desire and safety and privacy."

As the debate continues over the best legislative fixes, essentially all the researchers Scientific American spoke to agree on one idea: more information about these platforms can help us figure out exactly how they're causing harm. To that end, KOSA would mandate that the social media companies open up their closely held datasets to academics and nonprofits. "There's a lot we don't know," Hancock says, "because we're prevented."

If You Need Help

If you or someone you know is struggling or having thoughts of suicide, help is available. Call or text the 988 Suicide & Crisis Lifeline at 988 or use the online Lifeline Chat.

About the Author

Jesse Greenspan is a San Francisco Bay Area–based freelance journalist who writes about history and the environment.

COVID Can Cause Forgetfulness, Psychosis, Mania, or a Stutter

By Stephani Sutherland

P atrick Thornton, a 40-year-old math teacher in Houston, Texas, relies on his voice to clearly communicate with his high school students. So when he began to feel he was recovering from COVID, he was relieved to get his voice back a month after losing it. Thornton got sick in mid-August and had symptoms typical of a moderate case: a sore throat, headaches, trouble breathing. By the end of September, "I was more or less counting myself as on the mend and healing," Thornton says. "But on September 25, I took a nap, and then my mom called." As the two spoke, Thornton's mother remarked that it was great that his voice was returning. Something was wrong, however.

"I realized that some of the words didn't feel right in my mouth, you know?" he says. They felt jumbled, stuck inside. Thornton had suddenly developed a severe stutter for the first time in his life. "I got my voice back, but it broke my mouth," he says. After relaying the story over several minutes, Thornton sighs heavily with exhaustion. The thought of going back to teaching with his stutter, "that was terrifying," he says.

In November Thornton still struggled with low energy, chest pain, and headaches. And "sometimes my heart rate [would] just decide that we're being chased by a tiger out of nowhere," he adds. His stutter only worsened by that time, Thornton says, and he worried that it reflected some more insidious condition in his brain, despite doctors' insistence that the speech disruption was simply a product of stress.

A growing body of evidence warns that the legacy of the pandemic does not necessarily disappear when the novel coronavirus, or SARS-CoV-2, is cleared from the body. Among the millions of people who have survived respiratory complications from COVID-19, many still live with lingering symptoms in the wake of even a mild case of the disease. Neurological symptoms, ranging from fatigue to brain fog to loss of smell, persist after the virus is gone from the body.

An early survey of 153 COVID-19 patients in the U.K. and a more recent preprint study of people hospitalized with the disease in Italy both found that about a third had neurological symptoms of some kind. Other estimates have trended even higher. "There's a really wide spectrum of [neurological] manifestations of COVID," says Thomas Pollak, a neuropsychiatrist at King's College London and a co-author of the U.K. study. "Some are totally devastating, like stroke or encephalitis, and some are much more subtle." Increasingly common symptoms include fatigue and memory problems—and, at times, new cases of psychosis or mania.

Some neurological manifestations of post-COVID, such as stuttering, are more bizarre than others. But Houston's Thornton is not the only one afflicted. Soo-Eun Chang, a neuroscientist at the University of Michigan, is among the few researchers investigating stutter. "While stress and anxiety are not the cause of stutter, they do exacerbate it," Chang says, and that is true for Thornton. But she says the origins of the disorder lie in complex circuits of the brain that coordinate the millions of neuronal connections needed for human speech.

While most people develop this disruption of speech when they learn to talk, around age two, neurogenic stutter can arise after brain trauma, such as an injury. Chang says her colleagues in clinical practice have reported seeing an increase in cases of stuttering during the pandemic—mostly in people whose existing stutter worsened or whose childhood stutter returned.

Having the virus, she says, could lead to conditions that disrupt speech. "Speech is one of the more complex movement behaviors that humans perform," Chang says. "There are literally 100 muscles involved that have to coordinate on a millisecond time scale, so it's a significant feat. And it depends on a well-functioning brain." COVID's inflammatory response could undermine the efficiency of these circuits. "An immune-mediated attack on synaptic connections could lead to a change in brain function," she says.

The idea that SARS-CoV-2 can get into the human brain is mainly supported by autopsy studies, such as one by Frank Heppner, a neuropathologist at Charité–University Medicine Berlin, and his colleagues. The researchers found evidence of the virus in specific areas of the brain, probably near the sites of entry. One could be the lining of the nasal passage, the olfactory mucosa, which is in close contact with neuronal cells that could provide a route to the brain. "We started at that region and then physically mapped [a pathway through] the regions up to the olfactory bulb and further to brain stem nuclei," Heppner says. The researchers found evidence of viral protein in those distant brain stem regions but not in other areas of the brain. "This told us, or made it likely, that the virus used the transmucosal route along the olfactory nerve as a port of entry," Heppner adds.

They also saw viral particles in trigeminal nerves, which are sensory nerves that enter the brain and transmit the pain of headache. Heppner says his team also discovered hints that the virus could get into the brain through blood vessels. But autopsies were undertaken in those with severe disease, and it is uncertain whether the virus gets into the brain in milder cases. For most people, the symptoms brought on by COVID are likely the result of immune system activity. "The virus gets cleared from the lungs, but the immune system is triggered and doing harmful things," Heppner says. "The same could be true for the central nervous system. It's a fair speculation. It could explain very well the long COVID symptoms like chronic fatigue and problems in concentration."

William Banks, who studies the blood-brain barrier (BBB) at the Department of Veterans Affairs Puget Sound Health Care System in Washington State and the University of Washington Medical School, says, "The virus doesn't have to get into the brain to muck up function. We know there's a big cytokine storm," meaning the release of inflammatory signals by immune cells in serious cases. Even mild cases provoke cytokine release, however. And Banks says it is well established that "cytokines can cross the blood-brain barrier and cause depressionlike symptoms." Researchers refer to those symptoms—including a loss of interest in life, an increased desire to rest and sleep, and cognitive impairments—as "sickness behavior," which often accompanies a flu or cold. Those symptoms could drag on if cytokines continue to be released after the infection has passed.

Yet another possibility is that the virus itself does not cross the BBB but that a viral protein, perhaps shed from a dying virus, might do so. Banks and his colleagues showed as much in a recent paper in *Nature Neuroscience*. They injected mice with S1, which makes up half of SARS-CoV-2's "spike" protein, and found that it readily crossed the BBB. Michelle Erickson, who works with Banks at the VA Puget Sound and the University of Washington Medical School, says that the work "adds, at least in mice, a defined route by which the virus can get into brain, importantly, in the absence of inflammation," when the blood-brain barrier might be leaky. "We saw that spike can get into the intact BBB," she adds. "Often infiltration is almost entirely due to BBB disruption. But here it was only slightly disrupted, which was quite surprising to us."

The results hint that not only the S1 protein but potentially the virus itself could cross the BBB. A viral protein could cause damage by binding to proteins on neurons and other critical brain cells. "We know these binding proteins are very neurotoxic; they're stress inducing," Banks says. And the presence of any viral material could "shoot off the immune system."

There is yet another possibility: the virus could lead the immune system to produce damaging autoantibodies. These proteins bind not only to the virus but to other proteins in the body as well, either disrupting their function directly or triggering an immune attack on cells. "COVID wreaks havoc with the immune system," says neuropsychiatrist Pollak. "There's a huge surge in various inflammatory mediators." Some early evidence suggests that anti-SARS-CoV-2 antibodies may react to tissues in the brain and body, he says, and that could possibly occur at neurons.

43

Autoantibodies are the culprit in a recently described neurological disease called anti-NMDA receptor encephalitis, which can cause fatigue, brain fog, and even psychosis and coma. The immune system proteins bind to NMDA receptors that are critical for neuronal signaling. "Binding to neuronal proteins tends to disrupt synaptic function, like in the case of anti-NMDA receptor antibodies," Pollak says. "That leads to signaling dysfunction, and information processing gets out of whack."

The autoantibody hypothesis still warrants further research. "It's probably the most speculative and the one we know the least about," Banks says. Fatigue, brain fog, and other symptoms probably arise from multiple different immune-mediated mechanisms. But researchers agree that synapses, where brain signals are passed from neuron to neuron, are probably disrupted. "We're a long way off from understanding exactly how these nebulous responses arise," Pollak says. "But the general principle is that if you create a perturbation in the system or the brain, you'll affect its computational ability."

Recent preprint work by Andrew Yang at the laboratory of Tony Wyss-Coray of Stanford University also hints that the brain undergoes widespread changes in the wake of COVID-19 that could contribute to neurological symptoms. Yang and his colleagues found altered patterns of genes switching on and off in cells from the brains of patients who had died of the disease. These differences were observed in neurons and other brain cells—glia and immune cells called microglia. The genetic activation patterns differed from those observed in people who died of the flu or nonviral causes.

Yang's team examined an area of the cortex and saw dramatic gene expression changes in neurons in a specific region called cortical layer 2/3. These neurons have been recently implicated as playing a pivotal role in the complex processing required for human thought, so disruption of their activity could lead to mental fuzziness.

The patterns of genetic changes the researchers saw in the cortex mirrored genetic pathways mapped out in mental illnesses such as schizophrenia and depression. In addition, Yang also found gene-expression changes in microglia, which clean up waste and eat dead cells in a process called phagocytosis. Microglia can consume, or phagocytose, neuron bodies and synapses, reshaping neural circuits if the cells are dying or even when they are under stress. Neurons generally do not regenerate, so cognitive function may be impaired.

It is not only neurological symptoms that afflict patients. More common mental illnesses are affecting people with COVID, too. A study published in the Lancet Psychiatry showed that having the disease led to greater risk for anxiety, depression, and sleep disorders. Paul Harrison of the University of Oxford and his colleagues sifted through the electronic health records of nearly 70 million Americans and identified more than 62,000 people who had been diagnosed with COVID-19. In the three months following diagnosis, "we found that COVID was associated with roughly twice the incidence of common psychiatric diagnoses, compared with other health conditions," Harrison says.

Why COVID increased the risk for mental illness remains unclear. But Harrison says the virus itself is probably not directly responsible. He points to the psychological consequences of having a potentially fatal illness that could prevent you from returning from the hospital to your family. "There are all sorts of acute stresses associated with the diagnosis," he says. "I think those factors are going to be the most important explanation for the association we observed." Still, Harrison adds that the immune response provoked by the virus may have also had an effect on the brain that could have triggered psychiatric symptoms. He has a study underway to investigate the longer-term mental health effects of COVID-19, including symptoms such as brain fog and fatigue.

The legacy of COVID will undoubtedly persist. Although Thornton was still struggling by December, his stutter and energy level had improved, and he had gone back to teaching. "The kids have been really good about it," he says. "It's been a rocky road, but there's light at the end."

Still, the lasting effects could mean not just bothersome symptoms for a few people but a public mental health crisis, Banks says. "It could ultimately turn out that—as horrible as the death rate is, with perhaps one in 1,000 Americans having died—in the end there, could be this legacy affecting up to one in 10," he adds. "And it's probably rooted in neuroimmunity."

About the Author

Stephani Sutherland is a neuroscientist and science journalist based in southern California. She wrote about the causes of autoimmune diseases in our September 2021 issue. Follow her on X (formerly Twitter) @SutherlandPhD.

Climate Anxiety and Mental Illness

By Brian Barnett and Amit Anand

In mid-September, with much of the American West engulfed in flames, the National Oceanic and Atmospheric Administration announced that the Northern Hemisphere just experienced its hottest summer on record. Reports like this are increasingly common, and with each one climate change continues to morph from a vague notion of far-off future catastrophe to an unsettling reality unfolding before our eyes. While denial continues to hinder efforts to respond to climate change, nearly three fourths of Americans now think it's occurring, more than 60 percent believe it is caused by humans, and more than two thirds report they're at least "somewhat worried" by it.

Recently the term "climate anxiety" has crept into the lexicon to better describe our growing concerns about climate change. While there is evidence that climate anxiety can be identified and reliably measured, what's less clear is how it relates to mental illness. Mental health providers across the world are noting the presence of climate anxiety in their patients; however, the degree to which it is influencing mental illness is not yet clear, though evidence addressing this question is slowly growing.

For years now, mental health clinicians have seen climate anxiety influencing presentations of mental illness in a variety of ways, some extreme. For example, one case reported in the medical literature discusses a 17-year-old patient who was so concerned about climate change that he became delusional, believing that if he continued to drink water or use it for tasks at home, millions of people would soon die as a result of his consumption of their water supplies. Similarly, a study of individuals with obsessive-compulsive disorder found that nearly a third of individuals with OCD in Australia had compulsions focused on checking light switches, water taps, stoves, and other items to reduce their carbon footprint.

Recent studies are starting to look at links between climate anxiety and mental illness in larger samples to help better understand the directionality of their relationship. In a U.S. survey of more than 340 people published in 2018, climate concerns were associated with depressive symptoms. Ecological coping, which includes proenvironmental behaviors such as reducing energy consumption, appeared to be protective against depression, indicating climate concerns and poor coping skills to address them could be causing depressive symptoms. In Tuvalu, an island country in the Pacific Ocean at significant risk of being devastated by climate change in the near future, a survey published this year found that 87 percent of respondents reported such severe climate anxiety it impaired their ability to perform at least one activity of daily living. Such high rates of debilitating distress in this group suggest that individual populations will likely see more mental illness stemming from concerns about climate change as its repercussions draw nearer to them.

So who might be more vulnerable to mental illness secondary to the uncertainties around climate change? Unsurprisingly, climate anxiety appears higher in individuals with more concern about environmental issues at baseline and those already experiencing direct effects of climate change. Climatologists also face increased risk given their in-depth knowledge on the issue coupled with the frustrating task of trying to convey it to individuals and governments that often deny or downplay it. People with high levels of neuroticism, a personality trait that increases susceptibility to mental illness, are also likely to be at high risk.

Young people are a demographic of particular concern, since a recent national survey revealed that climate changes makes 57 percent of American teens feel afraid and 43 percent hopeless. There is an extensive generational gap in climate change concern, with younger individuals being more likely to believe climate change will pose a serious threat in their lifetimes. Young people also report more functional impairment secondary to climate anxiety than older people.

As younger people embrace with growing certainty the likelihood they could be inheriting a dying planet, many are so concerned they're considering not having children in order to reduce their carbon footprint. Their worries are especially alarming in light of growing suicide rates among adolescents and young adults, with a tripling of the rate among people aged 10–14 during 2007–2017. We don't know whether climate anxiety might be affecting suicide rates in this demographic, but the possibility of a connection demands ongoing vigilance and investigation.

The sociologist Émile Durkheim, who published the first extensive study of suicide in 1897, posited that many suicides happen when free-thinking individuals feel disconnected from society and there's a weakening of a society's regulatory institutions. Our current politically fueled controversy over climate change seems to present a perfect storm for increased suicidality as American youth grow distant from a society run by older political leaders, many of whom deny climate change altogether and even seek to weaken the scientific institutions whose very job it is to bring attention to it.

They've also seen activists from their ranks such as Greta Thunberg dismissed and even personally attacked by prominent leaders, demonstrating their concerns are being ignored outright. Climate anxiety among young people is likely greatly magnified by such behavior, given the sense of powerlessness it instills.

Some individuals report adaptive responses to climate anxiety like adopting proenvironmental behaviors and participating in collective action, while others are unable to respond behaviorally at all. It's not yet apparent how these varying reactions manifest on a population level and how they're influencing humanity's response to climate change. However, a recent survey of nearly 200 people found that, while climate anxiety was associated with an emotional response to climate change, it was not correlated with a behavioral response.

If this is true for humanity as a whole, we must urgently help motivate the anxious among us. Doing so successfully will require many approaches, such as delivering cognitive-behavioral therapy to the most severely affected to demonstrating to entire populations that change is possible by better publicizing productive efforts by organizations to reduce their carbon footprints. We can't let climate anxiety stop us from responding to climate change, because now, more than ever, we need action, not paralysis.

About the Authors

Brian Barnett, M.D., is a psychiatrist at Cleveland Clinic.

Amit Anand, M.D., is a psychiatrist at Cleveland Clinic.

Section 2: The Science of Mental Illness

Aggression Disorders Are Serious, Stigmatized, and Treatable

By Abigail Marsh

R oughly every month I receive an email from a parent somewhere in the world asking for help with a child who is violent, angry, or aggressive. Some people describe being physically beaten or having their life threatened by their son or daughter. These families may spend thousands of dollars on special schools and treatments. Often they are desperate, afraid and looking for guidance.

Psychologists recognize several conditions that are characterized by violence and aggression. They include conduct disorder and disruptive mood dysregulation disorder in children as well as antisocial personality disorder in adults. To this list I would add psychopathy, which is assessed using different criteria than those used to diagnose antisocial personality disorder—though it is not an official diagnosis in the fifth edition of the *Diagnostic and Statistical Manual of Mental Disorders*.

Although each of these conditions differs from the others in important ways, all are defined by the fact that affected individuals engage in persistent, severe antisocial, or aggressive behaviors. Children diagnosed with conduct disorder or disruptive mood dysregulation disorder, for example, may be physically violent or display bursts of destructive anger. These disorders, which are characterized by patterns of exploitative, hurtful, or cruel behavior, place children at risk for developing antisocial personality disorder or psychopathy when they grow up.

These disorders are not rare. Conduct disorder affects up to 9 percent of girls and up to 16 percent of boys. Its symptoms, such as stealing and deliberately harming people or animals, are among the most common reasons for referring children for mental health treatment. And antisocial personality disorder is estimated to affect one in 50 people, making it more prevalent than schizophrenia, bipolar disorder, or anorexia.

Given the prevalence and severity of these conditions, you might think abundant resources exist to help affected adults and children, but that is not the case. Relative to other common, serious mental disorders, disorders of aggression are underdiagnosed, undertreated, and underrecognized. And that is not because these disorders cannot be accurately diagnosed and successfully treated— they can. New research is providing clinicians and scientists more insight than ever before into how these conditions develop and how to intervene. And the earlier in life treatment begins, the more successful it tends to be.

But these disorders are terribly stigmatized, leading well-meaning clinicians to avoid diagnosing them and many patients and parents to refuse to accept them. The fact that generations of psychologists have invoked unhelpful moralistic frameworks— essentially condemning people with these disorders as "bad" or even "evil"—has only added to the intense negative judgment of these conditions. Even some mental health organizations, both private and public, avoid mentioning them.

We now know, however, that these disorders are true illnesses that reflect dysfunctional patterns of brain structure and function that lead to maladaptive thoughts and emotions and ultimately aggressive or violent behavior. These problems result from the combined influence of genetic risk factors and environmental stressors. Contrary to previous assumptions, they are not simply the result of "bad parenting"—an idea that has brought harm and shame to families. Varied factors, including birth complications, trauma, and exposure to toxins such as lead, may contribute—though for many people, no clear stressor is ever identified. In addition, without treatment, these disorders will likely persist or worsen.

Symptoms often emerge early in life and continue over time. A study conducted by researchers in Cyprus, Belgium, and Sweden and published last May tracked more than 2,000 children over the course of 10 years, collecting parent and teacher reports at five different time points between the ages of three and 13. The analysis revealed that an early emerging risk factor for later antisocial behavior was a fearless temperament, which often manifests as insensitivity to risk or harm in preschool-aged children. That trait can make children very difficult to parent because they do not learn to avoid risky, dangerous behaviors or behaviors that could result in punishment.

Perhaps unsurprisingly, the study also found that children with this temperament tended to experience harsher parenting and more conflict with their parents over time. They also developed "callous-unemotional traits," such as low empathy and remorse, which can further increase the risk for antisocial behaviors. Fearless temperaments may lead to low empathy in part because children who themselves do not feel fear strongly struggle to empathize with this emotion in others. Over time, "maladaptive fearlessness" can increase the risk of antisocial and criminal behavior in adulthood.

Given these tendencies, punishment does not improve behavior in children and adults with these illnesses. In fact, disorders characterized by aggression are often linked to *less responsiveness* to punishment, no matter how harsh, making it a futile response to aggression. Last July researchers in Germany, the U.K., and the Netherlands published findings from an experiment that examined how 92 children and adolescents with conduct disorder learned from punishment, compared with 130 of their typically developing peers. The children played a simple game in which they had to learn to select images that would result in a reward (gain of points) versus punishment (loss of points). As the game progressed, most children learned to avoid the images that result in punishment. But those with conduct disorder persisted in choosing these images more often, despite showing normal rates of learning from reward. This suggests that fundamental neurodevelopmental deficits in learning about punishment and risk underlie the emergence of serious antisocial behavior.

Though harsh punishment is ineffective for treating disorders of aggression, there are interventions that do help. In March 2023 another group published an analysis that pooled data from

60 studies that assessed the success of treatment for children with serious disruptive behavior disorders such as conduct disorder. The findings revealed that a range of treatment types were effective in improving children's symptoms—contrary to the prevalent myth that these disorders are untreatable.

The most effective approaches for severely affected children (those with callous-unemotional traits) were focused on training parents. In such treatments, which include parent management training and parent-child interaction therapy, therapists teach parents to use specific therapeutic techniques to reduce children's symptoms and improve their social skills and relationships. Consistent with the research on rewards and punishment, the therapeutic approaches that emphasize rewarding desired behaviors—and withholding rewards when children act out—are most effective. In general, these types of treatments should be considered first-line therapy for children with antisocial behavior, although too often they are not offered to families who could benefit from them.

Even the most seriously affected adults can improve with evidence-based treatment. A study published last year examined the effects of a treatment called schema therapy on more than 100 people convicted of violent offences in Dutch high-security forensic hospitals. All of these people had diagnoses of personality disorders such as antisocial personality disorder or narcissistic personality disorder. Schema therapy involves identifying and replacing maladaptive patterns of thinking, feeling, and relating to others. Patients treated with this therapy showed more improvement in their symptoms and moved more rapidly through rehabilitation than those who received standard individual or group therapy. This work suggests that rehabilitation is possible and could yield enormous potential savings in costs related to incarceration, as well as significant gains in public health and safety.

Of course, all of these treatments hinge on accurate diagnosis. My colleagues and I have found that children diagnosed with conduct disorder and callous-unemotional traits (which are also called "limited prosocial emotions") show *opposite* patterns of brain dysfunction compared with children who have conduct disorder as a result of anxiety or trauma. This finding indicates that these groups of kids would likely benefit from completely different treatments, despite some overlap in their symptoms, which brings us back again to the urgent need to improve the recognition, discussion, and accurate diagnosis of these disorders.

Many different steps are needed. For one, all major mental health organizations must give recognized disorders of aggression explicit parity with other mental disorders. Even today, someone who seeks information about conduct disorder, psychopathy, or antisocial personality disorder may search the websites of major organizations such as the National Institute of Mental Health or the National Alliance on Mental Illness in vain. This information gap was a major reason my colleagues and I came together to found Psychopathy Is, an organization dedicated to providing information and resources about psychopathy, a major contributor to many forms of antisociality in both children and adults, including bullying, domestic assault, and gun violence.

In addition, much more can be done to improve professional training and guidelines. And public and private mental health organizations must devote as many resources to screening tools, interventions, and studies of the causes of disorders of aggression as they do to similarly common and serious disorders, such as autism and attention deficit hyperactivity disorder. With more research will come better understanding, better treatments, and hope for a full and productive life for affected children and adults. Though these changes wouldn't yield instantaneous gains, they would represent a more compassionate and—most importantly—more effective approach to helping people, including the many families in need of answers.

This is an opinion and analysis article, and the views expressed by the author or authors are not necessarily those of Scientific American.

About the Author

Abigail Marsh is a psychologist and neuroscientist at Georgetown University, where she directs the Laboratory on Social & Affective Neuroscience.

Mania May Be a Mental Illness in Its Own Right

By Simon Makin

I n October 1997, at the age of 58, David Ho had an unusual experience while listening to a recording of Bach. "I began to dance and pretended to conduct," he says. "And as I practiced, instead of following the music, I felt as if I were creating it. I entered into a state of selfless oblivion, like a trance. My mind exploded. Flashes of insight rained down, and I saw beauty everywhere, in faces, living things and the cosmos. I became disinhibited, spontaneous, liberated."

Ho was in the grips of his first episode of mania. His description sounds like an enviable burst of creative energy, but the symptoms of mania can also include inflated self-esteem, grandiosity, racing thoughts, extreme talkativeness, decreased need for sleep, increased activity or agitation, reckless behavior, delusions, and other psychotic events. Severe episodes can impair day-to-day functions, sometimes enough to require hospitalization.

Perhaps the most surprising thing about such cases is that in the eyes of the psychiatric profession, mania does not exist as a distinct and unalloyed condition. Mania is usually known as the upside of bipolar disorder. For most people, it occurs alongside periods of depression, the downside. But Ho, who has had at least 20 manic episodes since 1997, has never suffered from depression. Thousands of people in the U.S. share that experience. Unlike those who experience only depression, however, patients with mania alone are lumped with those who have bipolar disorder. This puts psychiatry in the strange position of claiming that depression by itself is different from depression accompanied by mania but that mania by itself is not.

Most psychiatrists agree unipolar mania exists, but there is debate about whether it differs sufficiently from bipolar disorder in important enough ways to warrant a distinct diagnosis. Central to that debate is the tension in psychiatry between fewer, broader categories and more numerous, tightly defined ones. But the missing diagnosis may have consequences for patients: some studies suggest that people with unipolar mania may respond differently to certain treatments. If, as some researchers believe, unipolar mania and bipolar disorder differ in their underlying biology, classifying mania separately could speed the development of new treatments that are more personalized and effective. But because unipolar mania is far less common than bipolar disorder, research into the condition has been both scant and equivocal.

As both a patient and a clinical psychologist, Ho is well placed to advance this debate. In 2016 he published a self-study in the journal *Psychosis* cataloguing his symptoms, which include enhanced recall, increased empathy, and spiritual experiences. He has suffered some ill effects, including severe fatigue, confusion, and behavior that caused concern among friends and colleagues: he once burst into tears while delivering a lecture. But his professional training has helped him control his impulses and avoid delusional thinking. On balance, he believes that his madness, as he calls it, has enriched rather than damaged his life. "I'm aware my case may be atypical," Ho says. "Precisely for this reason, it challenges prevailing psychiatric beliefs that fail to acknowledge the positive value of mental disorders."

A Modern Illness

Credit for the modern concept of bipolar disorder usually goes to 19th-century French psychiatrist Jean-Pierre Falret, who called it *folie circulaire*, or "circular insanity," for its periods of pathologically elevated and depressed moods, usually separated by symptom-free periods of varying length. This idea became gospel in the early 20th century, when a father of modern psychiatry, Emil Kraepelin, proposed a historically significant hypothesis.

At the time, psychiatry drew a distinction between so-called reactive psychoses, which were seen as a response to outside events, and endogenous psychoses, which were innate. Kraepelin divided all endogenous psychoses into two broad classes: dementia praecox—now known as schizophrenia—and manic-depressive insanity, now known as bipolar disorder. Endogenous depression was therefore classed as a form of manic-depressive insanity. All mania also fell under the same rubric because mania was thought never to be a reaction to outside events. There were dissenters, notably the renowned German neurologist Carl Wernicke, who held that mania was related to hyperactivity of neural firing and depression to decreased neural activity. But Kraepelin's idea dominated and persists in today's diagnostic system.

The question of what to include under the umbrella of bipolar disorder reignited in 1966. In separate investigations, psychiatrists Carlo Perris of Umeå University in Sweden and Jules Angst of the University of Zurich in Switzerland each studied some 300 patients with either true bipolar disorder or depression alone and more than 2,000 of their close relatives.

Both researchers found that relatives of the bipolar patients had more mood disorders than those of patients with depression alone. They also discovered that although bipolar illness was common in the relatives of bipolar patients, it was no more common in relatives of depressed patients than in the general population. These findings, Perris and Angst argued, suggested that bipolar disorder and depression were genetically different conditions.

As a consequence, when the third edition of the *Diagnostic and Statistical Manual of Mental Disorders*, or *DSM*, appeared in 1980, it included major depressive disorder as a condition distinct from bipolar disorder. Perris and Angst's studies focused only on depression and did not address mania. "There weren't enough cases of pure mania to do anything reasonable," Angst says.

Whether unipolar mania should have its own diagnosis is complicated by bipolar disorder's clinical diversity. The manic and depressive phases vary in severity and the extent that one or the other dominates. The pattern of episodes varies unpredictably and from patient to patient. Mixed states, involving aspects of opposite mood extremes simultaneously, sometimes occur, too. Indeed, many psychiatrists argue that mood disorders are best thought of as lying on a spectrum, ranging from major depression through various bipolar presentations to pure mania.

In Search of a Subtype

The variability of symptoms, along with findings from large psychiatric genetics studies that implicate numerous biological factors, suggests that bipolar disorder includes a range of subtly different conditions. "One reason we still have limited understanding of bipolar disorder after 50 years of intense research is that it's treated as one entity, and it's clearly not," says psychiatrist Paul Grof of the University of Toronto.

The resistance to subtyping may be the result in part of changes in research funding over the past few decades, as the pharmaceutical industry has taken over progressively more psychiatric research from universities, Grof says. Drug companies generally just want to know if a new drug is better than a placebo, and the larger the patient group, the greater the likelihood of finding a significant difference. Subdividing bipolar disorder into smaller populations would complicate these efforts. The industry also prefers to study diagnoses recognized by the Food and Drug Administration—and unipolar mania is not on its list.

Institutional inertia can also come into play. Every rewrite of the *Diagnostic and Statistical Manual of Mental Disorders* is a laborious process. Each edition is based on the previous one, and any change must be backed by fresh evidence, with papers submitted to committees justifying the decision. The last edition, *DSM-5*, was published in 2013, and in the view of the committee tasked with reviewing mood disorders, unipolar mania was covered by the bipolar diagnosis known as BP-I, which is mania with or without associated depression. "There was very limited discussion as to whether mania should be separate because the onset and course of illness weren't seen as that different from BP-I," says psychiatrist Trisha Suppes of Stanford University, who was a member of the *DSM-5* work group for mood disorders.

The lack of a separate diagnosis may be making evidence harder to gather. The standardized clinical interview used under the *DSM* to make diagnoses for research studies has no category for unipolar mania, meaning investigations of the condition would have to rely on ad hoc techniques that might not align with those used in other studies. Unipolar mania is thus at the hub of a catch-22: the absence of a diagnosis is an impediment to research, and the paucity of research makes the creation of a diagnosis less likely.

In studies that do occur, the lack of a formal designation for unipolar mania makes it difficult to compare results. "A major problem is definitions," says Allan Young, a psychiatrist at King's College London. One source of disagreement is the severity of symptoms necessary for a case to qualify as mania. Another is the frequency of episodes. Some studies include anybody who has had at least one episode of mania with no history of depression, whereas others require three or four. Still others stipulate a minimum number of years of illness. These differences have led to widely disparate prevalence estimates for unipolar mania, ranging from 1.1 to 65.3 percent of patients with bipolar disorder.

Most of the studies completed so far also have methodological problems. The bulk are retrospective, in which researchers simply ask participants to recount past experiences—a process known to underestimate depression, perhaps inflating estimates of pure mania. Prospective studies that follow patients for years and include periodic assessments are better. "What you really want is someone who's lived their whole life, had multiple episodes of mania, and never had depression," Young says. "The first lady I saw like this died in her late 60s and had her first episode at 21, which is getting on for 50 years, so that's very convincing."

One of the longest prospective studies, led by David Solomon, now professor emeritus at Brown University, began in 1978 and was published in 2003. It began as a study of 229 bipolar patients, 27 of whom had mania with no history of depression. The investigators followed those 27 patients for up to 20 years; seven of them remained free of depression throughout the period. The results suggest that of the original 229 patients, 3 percent had unipolar mania. Solomon does not advocate the creation of a separate diagnosis for unipolar mania unless future research establishes differences in genesis, prognosis, or treatment response. But if the rate reported in the study held for the general population, the number of people with unipolar mania in the U.S. would be around 100,000—and there would be hundreds of thousands more worldwide.

The stories of people with unipolar mania help to explain why some researchers are convinced that the disorder is a separate entity. Lindsey, a ski coach from Portland, Me., is one such case. She was 18 when she had her first experience of mania. Eighteen years later she has never been depressed, yet she still has a diagnosis of bipolar disorder. "I'm the happiest person I know," she says. "I never accepted my diagnosis." As a result, she rejected treatment and continued to have episodes. She has been hospitalized five times and has landed in jail more than once.

Lindsey's episodes start with euphoria but can spiral into delusions and difficulty speaking. While manic, she feels no fatigue, hunger, or pain. One such episode, in her late 20s, began on a hike in New Mexico when she was overcome by a vision that the world was coming to an end. Lindsey called her father, who flew out to meet her and drive her home to Maine. "She had medication," her father says. "She just wasn't taking it." Early in the morning on an overnight stop in Nashville, Lindsey started playing the piano in the hotel lobby. An employee called the police, and Lindsey fled in the car.

In the adventure that followed, she deliberately got lost, buried her possessions near a railroad track, and abandoned the car. She then hopped a freight train, got off in the middle of rural Tennessee, climbed out of a rock-walled valley, and wandered into a chapel, where the pastor was able to glean enough information to contact her family. Shortly after resuming the drive home, Lindsey ran away from her father at a highway rest stop and started picking daisies in a fenced-off electrical area. The police were called again, and although the officer urged her to leave with her father, she insisted on being arrested.

In her cell, a guard pepper-sprayed her, and she ended up in the office of the jail's counselor. Lindsey was barely able to speak at this point, but she wrote "unipolar" repeatedly on a blackboard. The counselor then read Lindsey a description of mania. She credits this encounter as the moment she accepted the need to take medication. The counselor gave her Zyprexa (olanzapine), an antipsychotic. She recovered and takes it to this day, though not without reservations. "My medication is like a dose of sadness, hunger, fatigue, and pain," she says. Lindsey was euphoric throughout her ordeal, even while being pepper-sprayed. Only the people around her suffer. "I feel like I've been blessed with this illness that makes me so happy," she says, "but I feel selfish because of how it affects my family."

Lindsey married Andy, a journalist, in 2015, not long after he witnessed her last hospitalization. "It made the relationship stronger in the end," he says. "I got to see her as she clawed her way back to sanity. It was impressive." The most important factor in her treatment is whether a physician accepts that she is not bipolar. "When that's ignored, she no longer trusts that person," Andy says.

It All Gets Real

A curious quirk in the tale of this neglected disorder is that prevalence estimates vary worldwide and are consistently higher in non-Western countries. After qualifying in South Africa in 1997, psychiatrist Christoffel Grobler worked in an inpatient unit in Ireland, where his bipolar patients were mostly in depressed states. When Grobler returned to South Africa in 2009, he noticed the opposite pattern: his patients were mostly in manic states. To investigate, in 2010 he and his colleagues interviewed 103 bipolar patients in three hospitals, using a standard diagnostic questionnaire. They found that 32 percent of patients qualified as unipolar, defined as having at least five manic episodes over four or more years. "When I present this at conferences, people come up and say, 'We see this all the time,'" Grobler says.

Regional variations are tricky to interpret because cultural differences come into play: depression is more likely to be considered part of normal life in Africa, for example. The quality and procedures of health-care systems differ, and other causes, including infection or intoxication, may be a factor. But Grobler is convinced the geographical differences are genetic in origin and that unipolar mania therefore represents a distinct condition.

Getting to the bottom of this question will require large, multicultural international studies. In the meantime, scientists are trying to compensate for a shortage of data. One reason most early studies failed to find differences between mania and bipolar disorder may be that they are so slight that they can be reliably detected only in large samples. Now in his 90s, Angst addressed this problem by consolidating data from nine epidemiological studies conducted in the U.S., Germany, Switzerland, Brazil, and Holland. That study, published online in November 2018 in *Bipolar Disorders*, found that people with unipolar mania were more likely to be male but less likely to have attempted suicide or to suffer from anxiety, drug use, and eating disorders. Angst and his colleagues claim these findings suggest unipolar mania "should be established as a separate diagnosis."

Some of these findings align with three reviews of research on unipolar mania published in the past seven years. All three found that unipolar mania is less likely to co-occur with anxiety (which often accompanies depression) but more likely to come with psychotic symptoms. Unipolar mania also seems to confer less social impairment and involve fewer recurrences and better remission rates than bipolar disorder.

Perhaps most important, people with unipolar mania show subtle differences in their response to drugs administered as part of preventive treatment. Three studies found that patients with unipolar mania respond less well to lithium (a mood stabilizer and first option for bipolar) than those with true bipolar disorder do.

One of these studies, published in 2012 by Olcay Yazici and Sibel Çakir, then both at Istanbul University, also examined the question of whether unipolar mania is merely bipolar disorder weighted to the manic end of the spectrum—so-called dominant manic polarity. They divided 121 patients into two groups, 34 with unipolar mania and 87 with classic bipolar disorder. As the earlier studies found, the unipolar group had a lower response rate to lithium, and their response to another frontline bipolar treatment, the anticonvulsant Depakote (divalproex sodium), was no different.

The researchers next grouped all 121 patients according to whether the majority of their episodes were manic or depressive and then created a further division of patients whose manic episodes accounted for at least 80 percent of the total. A smaller percentage of patients who had at least a majority of manic episodes responded to lithium than among patients who had more depressive episodes, and this difference was greater for patients whose mania put them in the 80 percent group. Most telling, when those with unipolar mania were excluded from this analysis, these differences disappeared, suggesting the treatment difference relates to unipolar mania and not to dominant manic polarity and thus implying that unipolar mania is its own entity.

The Way Ahead

Those who are opposed to a separate diagnosis sometimes point out that the mania in unipolar mania is indistinguishable from that in bipolar disorder. But the same is true of depression, and many studies have found differences in the brains of people with major depression compared with those of individuals with bipolar disorder. Future work that compares brains of people with unipolar mania and bipolar disorder might be just as revealing.

Biological and brain-imaging studies of unipolar mania are rare. But one from several decades ago gives clues to differences in physiology. A 1992 CT scan study led by Sukdeb Mukherjee of the Medical College of Georgia at Augusta University found that unipolar mania patients had smaller third ventricles (one of four interconnected cavities in the brain that let cerebrospinal fluid flow) than bipolar patients did.

This result is intriguing because subsequent studies found that bipolar patients who experienced multiple episodes have larger ventricles than people who are experiencing their first episode or healthy control subjects, a hint that enlarged ventricles may be linked to pathology. The implication that unipolar mania may not cause as much damage in the brain tallies with the better outcomes associated with the condition.

Creating a separate diagnosis for unipolar mania remains controversial. An interim step would be to recognize it as an official subtype of bipolar disorder. Such a move might encourage research and raise awareness among clinicians. "There's a mystery here we don't understand: Why do some people get mania and then depression, whereas others stay unipolar manic?" Suppes asks. "It's deserving of more research than it's gotten so far." Further investigation might also benefit patients who do not identify with other labels. Lindsey pleads, "The most important thing my doctor could do for me is say, 'I'm sorry, we were wrong—you're not bipolar, you're unipolar.'"

Psychic Fuel for the Creative Brain

The mad genius may be more than a cliché. Of all the tropes of artists and mental afflictions, the most enduring is the one of a genius in the throes of mania. Iconic figures ranging from William Blake to Ernest Hemingway to Kurt Cobain were known or believed to have bipolar disorder. The association has intuitive appeal: the euphoria, abundant energy, and racing thoughts of mania are credible fuel for creativity.

Scientific evidence for the association has mostly been inconclusive. Much of the data comes from historical sources, and most accounts are anecdotal. Modern investigative techniques have revealed surprisingly little about what happens in the brain during mania, partly because brain imaging requires minimal head movement, so scanning someone in a floridly manic state is a challenge. As a dynamic process involving the interplay of multiple brain networks, creativity is also difficult to research.

But comparing findings from research into bipolar disorder with certain studies of creativity reveals hints of a link: cognitive "disinhibition" seems to be a feature of both the creative state described as being in the "flow" and altered brain circuits in bipolar disorder.

Brain-imaging studies have found reduced activity in a part of the prefrontal cortex that helps to regulate emotion, which may be linked to impaired impulse control and extremes of mood in people with bipolar disorder. (The prefrontal cortex is the brain's "orchestra conductor" responsible for directing various mental processes.) Some of these studies have also found diminished activity in an area involved in suppressing the kind of spontaneous thought that appears to well up from the unconscious, seemingly out of nowhere.

These results are reminiscent of a 2008 study of improvising jazz musicians and a 2012 study of freestyling rappers, conducted by the team of speech neuroscientist Allen Braun, then at the National Institutes of Health, which found reduced activity in the part of the prefrontal cortex that inhibits spontaneous cognition. The researchers also found an increase in activity in a section of the prefrontal cortex that is part of the so-called default mode network, which revs up when a person is not focusing on a task but rather is imagining things or ruminating on the past. They believe what they observed reflects relaxation of focused attention and control, making way for a creative thought process in which inspiration bubbles up from the unconscious. Other studies have found reduced thickness of certain cortical regions in both creative and bipolar brains, which may be linked to altered brain activity and disinhibited cognition.

Another element in the thinking patterns of creative and manic people is the ability to make mental connections that elude others. Neuroscientist Nancy Andreasen of the University of Iowa has found that creative people show greater activity in the so-called association cortices, which are regions tasked with linking related elements of cognition. These brain areas are not devoted to processing specific sensory or motor functions but instead engage with tasks such as tying together a written word with its sound and meaning. Andreasen believes creative ideas probably happen when these types of associations occur freely in the brain during unconscious mental states, when thoughts become momentarily disorganized—not unlike psychotic states of mania.

This observation resonates with clinical psychologist David Ho, who has experienced racing thoughts and extraordinarily enhanced recall during manic episodes, letting him write without inhibition or self-doubt. "With repression vanished, my mind functioned with holistic oneness," he says. "Creative ideas rained down faster than I could cope." Researchers do not know if the association cortices are more active in mania, but all these findings suggest that at key moments of the creative process, our thought processes flow more freely, with novel combinations of sights, sounds, memories, meanings, and feelings producing insight and originality in creative work akin perhaps to what happens during mania.

Of course, mental illness is neither necessary nor sufficient for creative talent, and severe manic episodes most likely are too debilitating for any kind of sustained activity. But researchers have found that family members of people with bipolar disorder also tend to be more creative than average, supporting the idea that mild manifestations of the disorder may furnish cognitive benefits.

It is important not to romanticize conditions that mainly cause suffering, but evidence that mania can enhance creativity in some people may help reduce the stigma of a diagnosis. "It is possible to retain a measure of madness in dignified living," Ho says, "and of dignity even in a state of madness."

About the Author

Simon Makin is a freelance science journalist based in the U.K. His work has appeared in New Scientist, *the* Economist, Scientific American *and* Nature, *among others. He covers the life sciences and specializes in neuroscience, psychology and mental health. Follow Makin on X (formerly Twitter) @SimonMakin.*

Susceptibility to Mental Illness May Have Helped Humans Adapt over the Millennia

By Dana G. Smith

Nearly one in five Americans currently suffers from a mental illness, and roughly half of us will be diagnosed with one at some point in our lives. Yet, these occurrences may have nothing to do with a genetic flaw or a traumatic event.

Randolph Nesse, a professor of life sciences at Arizona State University, attributes high rates of psychiatric disorders to natural selection operating on our genes without paying heed to our emotional well-being. What's more, the selective processes took place thousands of years before the unique stresses of modern urban existence, leading to a mismatch between our current environment and the one for which we were adapted.

In his new book, *Good Reasons for Bad Feelings: Insights from the Frontier of Evolutionary Psychiatry,* Nesse recruits the framework of evolutionary medicine to make a case for why psychiatric disorders persist despite their debilitating consequences. Some conditions, like depression and anxiety, may have developed from normal, advantageous emotions. Others, such as schizophrenia or bipolar disorder, result from genetic mutations that may have been beneficial in less extreme manifestations of a trait. *Scientific American* spoke to Nesse about viewing psychiatry through an evolutionary lens to help both patients and clinicians.

[An edited transcript of the interview follows.]

Q: A big part of your thesis is that some traits of mental disorders can be advantageous or adaptive—a depressed mood, for instance, might be beneficial for us. Where do you draw the line between the normal spectrum of emotion and pathology?

A: You can't decide what's normal and what's abnormal until you understand the ordinary function of any trait—whether it's vomiting or cough or fever or nausea. You start with its normal function and in what situation it gives selected advantages. But there are a lot of places where natural selection has shaped mechanisms that express these defenses when they're not needed, and very often that emotional response is painful and unnecessary in that instance. Then there's a category of emotions that make us feel bad but benefit our genes. A lot of sexual longings [extramarital affairs or unrequited love], for instance, don't do us any good at all, but they might potentially benefit our genes in the long run.

So it's not saying that these emotions are useful all the time. It's the capacity for these emotions that is useful. And the regulation systems [that control emotion] were shaped by natural selection—so sometimes they're useful for us, sometimes they're useful for our genes, sometimes it's false alarms in the system and sometimes the brain is just broken. We shouldn't try to make any global generalizations, we should examine every patient individually and try to understand what's going on.

Q: In the book you suggest that low mood could be advantageous for two very separate reasons. One of the motivators is to shift strategies to escape a situation, and the other is to have people stop striving and conserve energy. How do you reconcile these opposing theories?

A: It's intuitively obvious that when an organism, not just a human, is wasting energy trying to pursue a goal and not making progress, it's best to wait and slow down and not waste energy. Then if nothing works—even when you try to find a new strategy—to give up that goal completely.

Of course for we humans, it's not always seeking out nuts and fruits and berries. We're trying to garner social resources, and that creates inordinate complexity and competition. And it's not so easy to give up looking for a marital partner or give up looking for a job; we can't just do that. These moods are guiding us to try to put effort into things that are going to work instead of things that are not going to work. That doesn't mean we should just follow them, but it does mean respecting them more and trying to figure out what they might be telling us about the things we're trying to do in life.

Q: Could treating someone with antidepressants be disadvantageous, then, if low mood is a normal coping mechanism?

A: Evolutionary psychology I see very much as a subset of evolutionary medicine in general. And one of the most practically useful insights of evolutionary medicine is that we should be analyzing the costs and benefits of blocking every single defensive response, whether it's fever or pain or nausea or vomiting or cough or fatigue. Usually because of the "smoke detector" principle you can block these things safely. [The principle is Nesse's theory that an overactive fight-or-flight response that causes false alarms—and potentially an anxiety disorder—is better than an underactive system that fails to alert you to danger and could result in death.]

Some people have said that because I say low mood can be useful, I think we shouldn't treat it with medications. I say exactly the opposite. Once you know that low mood is usually not helpful even though it's normal, you go ahead and relieve it however you can.

Q: You talk a lot about genes in the book, but also how we've come up short in looking for genes for depression or schizophrenia. What role do you think genes play in the evolutionary model of the mental illness?

A: First of all, there are two very different categories of illness that should be kept separate. One is the emotional disorders, which are potentially normal, useful responses to situations. And in all such responses, variability and sensitivity are influenced by lots of different genes.

There are also mental disorders that are the most severe ones that are just plain old genetic diseases: bipolar disease and autism and schizophrenia. They're genetic diseases, and whether you get them or not is overwhelmingly dependent on what genes you have. But why would a strong, inheritable trait that cuts fitness by half not be selected against? I think this is one of the deepest mysteries in psychiatry.

Q: What could be some of the potential benefit of these latter conditions or other uses for these genes?

A: For bipolar disease, the reduction in the number of offspring is not very great at all, so it might be that there's not much selection acting there. And what if a tendency to be bipolar resulted in having even more children? What would happen then? Well it [the gene] would become universal, even though it caused bipolar disease. Maybe something like this has already happened. Maybe many of us have tendencies to grand ambitions and mood swings that probably aren't good for us but might lend to grand successes on occasion, and that might lead to great reproductive success.

Then there's the "cliff edge" effect, which is the possibility that some traits are pushed very far towards a peak that's close to a place where fitness collapses for a few percent of the population. This could be a new way of looking at all of these diseases in which we have many genes with small effects. It might be that what we should be looking for is the fitness landscape and not assume that the genes involved are abnormal.

Q: What do you hope patients or clinicians can gain from reading your book?

A: I find many of my patients feel like they're abnormal if they are told, "You have an anxiety disorder, you have a depressive disorder." Talk with them a little bit about the fact that there are advantages to anxiety and that low moods might have meaning. It might not just be something that's broken in you, it might be that your emotions are trying to tell you something. I think that makes many people feel less like they're defective.

About the Author

Dana G. Smith is a freelance science writer specializing in brains and bodies. She has written for Scientific American, *the* Atlantic, *the* Guardian, NPR, Discover, *and* Fast Company, *among other outlets. In a previous life, she earned a Ph.D. in experimental psychology from the University of Cambridge.*

Analysis of a Million-Plus Genomes Points to Blurring Lines among Brain Disorders

By Emily Willingham

Is lower academic achievement in early life tied to the same gene changes as an increased risk for Alzheimer's in older age? That is one of dozens of possible deductions to be drawn from the largest genomic study of brain conditions ever conducted, research that obscures what often have been considered clear diagnostic borders.

According to the findings, published June 22 [2018] in *Science,* conditions such as schizophrenia, major depressive disorder (MDD), and bipolar disorder share a suite of overlapping genetic variants rather than having distinct genetic signatures.

In addition to the genetic links between educational attainment and Alzheimer's risk, the results link neuroticism to anorexia nervosa, anxiety disorders, MDD, and obsessive-compulsive disorder (OCD). Neurological disorders like Parkinson's and multiple sclerosis, however, have few variants in common with each other or with psychiatric conditions.

This mother lode of findings comes after a six-year delving into genomes representing more than a million people, a quest for unusual genetic signals that track with one or more of 42 disorders and traits.

Researchers from 600-plus institutions worldwide, grouped into 25 consortia, pooled their genomic data for the effort, dubbed the "Brainstorm Consortium." Their goal was to probe the immense data set for links among gene variants, brain disorders, and physical and cognitive traits.

And they found many, many links.

"One of the big messages is that psychiatric disorders turned out to be very connected on the genetic level," says Verneri Anttila, the first author on the paper and a postdoctoral research fellow at the Broad Institute. The implication is that "current diagnostics don't accurately separate the mechanisms" for the conditions, he says, which might be a factor in explaining the struggle to find new treatments.

But because the study was a "hypothesis-free approach," as Anttila describes it, showing only statistical associations among genes, not proof of a common genetic basis, the findings are only a starting point for digging deeper "to better understand how these disorders arise," he says.

To deliver this treasure trove of starting points, the Brainstorm Consortium applied a statistical method that teases out truly distinct signals from noise in the genome and tracked how those signals—small changes in DNA sequences that represent gene variants—associated with psychiatric and neurological diagnoses of 265,218 patients compared to 784,643 unaffected people.

Then, they looked at how variants that tracked with brain disorders related to educational achievement and physical and cognitive measures. Ultimately, the analysis involved 25 conditions, including MDD, autism, epilepsy, schizophrenia, post-traumatic stress disorder (PTSD), and migraine.

To spice it up a bit, the investigators also looked at 13 behavioral traits, including cognitive and personality measures, and four physical factors—Crohn's disease, vascular disease, height, and body mass index.

From this brew of inputs, the researchers extracted statistical links between genetic variants and different disorders and identified overlaps across almost all psychiatric conditions they examined. Schizophrenia, anxiety disorder, MDD, bipolar disorder, and attention deficit hyperactivity disorder (ADHD) all shared variants. Tourette syndrome, OCD, and MDD clustered together, as did anorexia nervosa, schizophrenia, and OCD.

Standing out from this crowd at the end of the shared-variant spectrum was schizophrenia, which overlapped with all of the psychiatric disorders except anxiety. PTSD, meanwhile, showed no significant association with any of them.

Although neurological disorders tended to remain distinct, an exception was migraine, which had many variants in common with ADHD, Tourette syndrome, and MDD. Migraine also was associated with the personality trait "neuroticism," which in turn overlapped with several psychiatric conditions, including MDD, OCD, and schizophrenia.

Crohn's disease, intended to represent immune disorders, had no variants in common with any other condition assessed, but vascular disease, stroke, and MDD had commonalities.

Some of these associations are surprising, and some are not, says John Hardy, chair of molecular biology of neurological disease at the University College London Institute of Neurology, who was not involved with the study. Hardy calls the study a "reliable and well-organized piece of work." The overlap among psychiatric diseases isn't a big shock, he says, because "they share symptoms and can sometimes be confused with each other."

What stands out for him is a lack of overlap between Alzheimer's and Parkinson's, both neurodegenerative conditions. Based on these findings, he says, "they really do seem distinct, which probably means that the mechanisms of cell death are different."

Anttila mentions a couple of other curveballs. "I was personally surprised by the lack of such correlations between neurological disorders and psychiatric ones," he says, noting that he would have expected depression, for example, to show overlap with some neurological diseases.

The other unexpected result for Anttila and his colleagues was the link between cognitive factors and the psychiatric and neurological disorders. "Having the genetic variants that predispose someone to Alzheimer's disease at age 70 to be significantly correlated with those predisposing them towards worse results in school at age 12 was definitely a surprise to us," he says.

Some of the non-overlapping results were unanticipated, too. Even though about a third of people with autism also have seizures, this probe of genomic information turned up little in the way of common variants between autism and epilepsy. Anttila says that this analysis was "one of the smaller ones" in the work, which might explain the lack of a link.

In fact, having fewer than 10,000 cases in any one of the many analyses in the study could have yielded misleading results because of the small sample size, not because there is no association, says Cathryn Lewis, professor of genetic epidemiology and statistics at King's College London. Lewis is a member of the U.K.'s Psychiatric Genomics Consortium and contributed samples to the study but was not involved in the analysis.

Another possible explanation for the lack of shared variants between autism and epilepsy is that the study focused on commonly occurring, but not on rare, candidates. "The methods are definitely sound, well-respected, and widely used," she says, but because they involve looking only at common variants, they won't capture rare ones.

With dozens of new investigative starting points involving these common variants in-hand, what's next? "The immediate takeaway from this study is that now that we have identified these connections, we can better understand how these disorders arise," says Anttila. "There may be some deeper genetic mechanisms at play here [that] predispose individuals to multiple disorders, rather than just a single one."

About the Author

Emily Willingham is a science writer and author of the books Phallacy: Life Lessons from the Animal Penis *(Avery, Penguin Publishing Group, 2020) and* The Tailored Brain: From Ketamine, to Keto, to Companionship: A User's Guide to Feeling Better and Thinking Smarter *(Basic Books, 2021).*

Mental Illness Is Far More Common Than We Knew

By Aaron Reuben and Jonathan Schaefer

Most of us know at least one person who has struggled with a bout of debilitating mental illness. Despite their familiarity, however, these kinds of episodes are typically considered unusual and even shameful.

New research, from our laboratory and from others around the world, however, suggests mental illnesses are so common that almost everyone will develop at least one diagnosable mental disorder at some point in their life. Most of these people will never receive treatment, and their relationships, job performance, and life satisfaction will likely suffer. Meanwhile the few individuals who never seem to develop a disorder may offer psychology a new avenue of study, allowing researchers to ask what it takes to be abnormally, enduringly mentally *well*.

Epidemiologists have long known that at any given time, roughly 20 to 25 percent of the population suffers from a mental illness, which means they experience psychological distress severe enough to impair functioning at work, at school, or in their relationships. Extensive national surveys, conducted from the mid-1990s through the early 2000s, had suggested that a much higher percentage, close to half the population, would experience a mental illness at *some point*.

These surveys were large, involving thousands of participants representative of the U.S. in age, sex, social class and ethnicity. They were also, however, *retrospective*, which means they relied on survey respondents' accurate recollection of feelings and behaviors months, years, and even decades in the past. Human memory is fallible, and modern science has demonstrated that people are notoriously inconsistent reporters about their own mental health history, leaving the final accuracy of these studies up for debate.

Of further concern, up to a third of individuals contacted by the national surveys failed to enroll in the studies. Other tests suggested that these "nonresponders" tended to have worse mental health.

A new study by one of us (Schaefer), published earlier this year in the *Journal of Abnormal Psychology* (whose very name suggests an outdated understanding of the prevalence of mental illness), took a different approach to estimating disease burden. Rather than asking people to think back many years, Schaefer and his colleagues instead closely followed one generation of New Zealanders, all born in the same town, from birth to midlife. They conducted in-depth check-ins every few years to assess any evidence of mental illness having occurred during the preceding year.

They found that if you follow people over time and screen them regularly using simple, evidence-based tools, the percentage of those who develop a diagnosable mental illness jumps to well more than 80 percent. In the cohort only 17 percent of study members did not develop a disorder, at least briefly, by middle age. Because Schaefer's team could not be certain that these individuals remained disorder-free in the years between assessments, the true proportion that never experienced a mental illness may be even smaller.

Put another way, the study shows that you are more likely to experience a bout of mental illness than you are to acquire diabetes, heart disease, or any kind of cancer whatsoever. These findings have been corroborated by data from similar cohorts in New Zealand, Switzerland, and the U.S.

If you ever develop a psychological disorder, many assume you will have it for life. The newest research suggests that for the most common psychological complaints, this is simply not true. "A substantial component of what we describe as disorder is often short-lived, of lesser severity or self-limiting," says John Horwood, a psychiatric epidemiologist and director of the longitudinal Christchurch Health and Development Study in New Zealand. (Horwood has found that close to 85 percent of the Christchurch study members have a diagnosable mental illness by midlife.)

This may be a useful message to spread. According to Jason Siegel, a professor of social psychology at Claremont Graduate University, people tend to be more sympathetic and helpful when they believe that a friend or coworker's health problems are temporary.

And individuals with mental illness need support. Even short-lived or self-limiting disorders can wreak havoc on a person's life. To be classified as having a disorder, "an individual typically has to meet fairly stringent symptom criteria," Horwood says. "There needs to be substantial impairment of functioning."

To some, though, the new statistics on mental illness rates can sound a lot like the overmedicalization of "normal" human experience. Advocates for people with mental health concerns tend to disagree with this perspective. "I'm not at all surprised by these findings," says Paul Gionfriddo, president of Mental Health America, a national advocacy group. His organization views mental illnesses as common, "though not always enduring." Three years ago Mental Health America launched a web-based tool to allow individuals to discreetly screen themselves for possible psychological disorders. Since then, the tool has been used for more than 1.5 million screenings, with more than 3,000 screens a day now used to determine if people may have a condition that could benefit from treatment.

The widespread nature of mental illness, unearthed by careful longitudinal research, holds some implications for the way we study and treat disease in this country. To Gionfriddo, a former lawmaker who watched his son end up homeless and incarcerated following undiagnosed childhood schizophrenia, "one implication of these new studies is that we as a society will get tremendous benefit out of ubiquitous mental health screening."

Although the U.S. Preventive Services Task Force currently recommends mental health screening on a regular basis for everyone older than 11 years, such screening is still far from routine. "At a time when we have recognized the importance of early intervention for cancer or for diabetes or heart disease, why would we say, 'OK, for mental illness, we aren't going to screen or do early intervention'?" Gionfriddo says. "This should be as common for adults as blood pressure screening. Putting our head in the sand and waiting for a catastrophe is not a health care plan."

Another implication stems from the fact that individuals who never develop a mental illness—those who experience what we call "enduring mental health"—are actually quite remarkable. These people may be the mental health equivalents of healthy centenarians: individuals who somehow manage to beat the odds and enjoy good health for much longer than we would expect. It is possible that studying the mentally robust more closely could provide insight into how we can help more people to enjoy lives like theirs.

Who are these extraordinary people? In Schaefer's New Zealand cohort, his team found that those with enduring mental health tended to have two things going for them: First, they had little to no family history of mental illness. Second, they tended to have what the researchers call "advantageous" personalities. As early as age five, individuals who would make it to midlife without an episode of mental disorder tended to display fewer negative emotions, get along better with their peers, and have greater self-control. Perhaps just as striking, the team found that these individuals were *not* any richer, smarter, or physically healthier than their peers, at least in childhood.

Ultimately the most important suggestion from the newest research is that mental health concerns may be nearly universal. As a result, society should begin to view mental illnesses like bone breaks, kidney stones, or common colds—as part of the normal wear and tear of life. Acknowledging this universality may allow us to finally devote adequate resources to screening, treating, and preventing mental illnesses. It may also help us go easier on ourselves and our loved ones when we inevitably hit our own rough patches in the road.

This article was published in Scientific American's *former blog network and reflects the views of the author, not necessarily those of* Scientific American.

About the Author

Aaron Reuben is a graduate student in clinical psychology at Duke University. He writes about nature, psychology, neuroscience and public health.

Jonathan Schaefer is a graduate student in clinical psychology at Duke and a Carolina Consortium on Human Development predoctoral fellow. He studies developmental psychopathology, psychiatric epidemiology and intelligence.

Getting to the Root of the Problem: Stem Cells Are Revealing New Secrets about Mental Illness

By Dina Fine Maron

Millions of Americans who suffer from bipolar disorder depend on lithium. The medication has been prescribed for half a century to help stabilize patients' moods and prevent manic or depressive episodes. Yet what it does in the brain—and why it does not work for some people—has remained largely mysterious.

But last year San Diego–based researchers uncovered new details about how lithium may alter moods, thanks to an approach recently championed by a small number of scientists studying mental illness: The San Diego team used established lab techniques to reprogram patients' skin cells into stem cells capable of becoming any other kind—and then chemically coaxed them into becoming brain cells.

This process is now providing the first real stand-ins for brain cells from mentally ill humans, allowing for unprecedented direct experiments. Proponents hope studying these lab-grown neurons and related cells will eventually lead to more precise and effective treatment options for a variety of conditions. The San Diego team has already used this technique to show some bipolar cases may have more to do with protein regulation than genetic errors. And another lab discovered the activity of glial cells (a type of brain cell that supports neuron function) likely helps fuel schizophrenia—upending the theory that the disorder results mainly from faulty neurons.

This new wave of research builds on Shinya Yamanaka's Nobel-winning experiments on cellular reprogramming from a decade ago. His landmark findings about creating induced pluripotent stem cells (iPSCs) have only recently been applied to studying mental illness as the field has matured. "What's really sparked that move now has been the ability to make patient-specific stem cells—and

84

once you can do that, then all sorts of diseases become amenable to investigation," says Steven Goldman, who specializes in cellular and gene therapy at the University of Rochester Medical Center.

To get to the bottom of why lithium helps some bipolar patients, stem cell scientist Evan Snyder and his colleagues at the Sanford Burnham Prebys Medical Discovery Institute wanted to examine neuron formation—comparing samples from those who respond to the medication and those who do not. The team obtained ordinary skin cells from people in both groups and transformed those samples into iPSCs and then brain cells. "When you reprogram cells into iPSCs they lose all markers of age, regardless of how old the person is," says Kristen Brennand, a stem cell biologist at the Icahn School of Medicine at Mount Sinai who was not involved in the work. "We can look at disease risk in a dish without any impact of things like drug abuse or adolescent trauma or infection of the mother while pregnant—so all we have is the genetic risk that was there when sperm met egg."

With these lab-grown models, Snyder and his team were able to compare how neurons matured in the two bipolar groups. They could also scour the cells' molecular pathways for possible explanations about how lithium works and why. They ultimately found that a protein called CRMP2, which regulates neural networks and is found inside of cells, appears to play an outsize role in influencing whether or not lithium helps patients.

Lithium, they concluded, makes CRMP2 act normally. Apparently the protein acts sluggishly in some bipolar patients, hampering neurons' ability to form dendritic spines—little bumps that occur on the edges of nerve cells that are necessary for neural communication. The problem, the researchers found, is not caused by an abnormal gene or errors in the responsiveness of a gene—or even the amount of protein a gene makes. Instead it stems from changes to the shape, weight, or electrical charge of the protein. This makes lithium-responsive bipolar disease the first confirmed mental health disorder fueled not by a genetic mutation but rather by hiccups in the "post-translational modification" of a protein, Snyder says. He suspects cases of bipolar disorder that do not respond to the drug actually comprise a different disease altogether.

Looking at these findings, researchers may now try to develop lithium alternatives that similarly restore CRMP2 activity, but only act on that protein pathway—allowing patients to avoid problematic side effects that may come from lithium hitting inappropriate targets. (It can, for example, cause memory deficits and fine-motor-skill deficiencies.) Researchers have previously had some information about the brain pathway lithium works on, but Brennand notes gaps have remained. "Evan has described another target of lithium, and this one might be more accurate," she says.

Creating Mini-Brains in the Lab

One problem in studying mental illness has always been that the brain is not very accessible while a patient is alive. Scientists have devised some ways around this: During the last decade genome-wide association studies have helped scientists link certain genetic mutations to specific disorders, for example. But that work left many mysteries about the causes of mental illnesses including schizophrenia, autism, and bipolar disorder, which are all related to many genes. Animal studies can often help but scientists cannot know if a mouse bred to have certain characteristics of schizophrenia is truly a schizophrenic mouse.

Work with induced pluripotent stem cells has helped change how clinicians think about schizophrenia. Goldman and some colleagues reported in August glial cells play a central role in the disorder. The researchers took iPSCs from schizophrenic and healthy subjects, turned them into glial progenitor cells, and showed that only the ones from the mentally ill patients would alter the behavior of mice implanted with them. These mice developed symptoms similar to those of some humans with schizophrenia, including reduced inhibition, social isolation, and excessive anxiety.

Tapping stem cells is particularly exciting because it can be coupled with traditional methods of studying mental illness, according to specialists in the field. For example, once researchers identify cells they think are significant, they can place them into mouse models (as Goldman did), seeing how they affect the behavior of these human-rodent chimeras. "In these cases, we are turning the mouse brain into a living test tube," Goldman says. He notes scientists can also compare cells from a schizophrenic patient and a mentally healthy patient, and look for anatomical differences. "These technologies have given us a leg up we didn't have years ago," he adds. Researchers are also coupling iPSCs with gene-editing techniques to create cell populations with specific genetic mutations— or to determine whether specific genetic mutations cause certain problems—says Guo-li Ming, a neuroscientist at the University of Pennsylvania Perelman School of Medicine.

Ming was one of the first researchers to employ iPSCs to explore mental health disorders. Lately she and others have also been taking the field in another direction: using iPSCs to develop 3-D brain organoid models, essentially building mini-brains comprising different neural cells. These cells live and interact in a solution, recapitulating many unique features of human brain development. This allows scientists to study the cross-talk among different types of cells in the brain, a process that may be involved in mental health disorders, Ming says.

The tantalizing goals of all of this stem cell work, she says, are to create personalized medications for individual patients and be able to quickly screen existing drugs against patients' cells in the lab—determining whether doctors should send patients home with specific drugs. "Maybe in a decade or two we can achieve at least some of this," Ming says. Yet already, Snyder says, the new findings have opened an "entirely new epoch in research."

About the Author

Dana Fine Maron, formerly an associate editor at Scientific American, *is now a wildlife trade investigative reporter at* National Geographic.

A New Way to Think about Mental Illness

By Kristopher Nielsen

H ave you ever heard of a condition known as "general paresis of the insane"? Probably not. In the 19th century general paresis was one of the most commonly diagnosed mental disorders. Its symptoms included odd social behaviors, impaired judgment, depressed mood, and difficulty concentrating. Around the turn of the 20th century, though, we figured what it really was—a form of late-stage syphilis infecting the brain and disrupting its function. A few decades later we discovered a highly effective treatment: penicillin.

Although general paresis is now very rare, its example is still instructive. Any honest researcher will tell you we don't currently have good explanations for most mental disorders. Depression, obsessive-compulsive disorder, schizophrenia—we don't really know how these patterns of disrupted thought, behavior, and emotion develop or why they stick around.

Yet the hope remains that, much like with general paresis, we may soon discover the root causes of these illnesses, and this knowledge may tell us how to treat them. An example of this hope can be seen in the popular notion that a "chemical imbalance" causes depression. This might turn out to be true, but the truth is we don't know.

Some researchers are starting to think that for many mental disorders, such hope might be based on incorrect assumptions. Instead of having one root cause, as general paresis did, mental disorders might be caused by many mechanisms acting together. These mechanisms might be situated in the brain, but they could also be located in the body and even in the external environment, interacting with one another in a network to create the patterns of distress and dysfunction we currently recognize and label as varieties of mental illness. In this more complex view, patterns such as depression and generalized anxiety arise as tendencies in the human brain-body-environment system. Once the patterns are established, they are hard to change because the network continues to maintain them.

If the causal structures of many mental disorders are complex, how should we seek to illuminate them? I think recognizing the complexity should push us to rethink how mental illness is studied.

For a start, we should no longer be looking for just one nugget of truth. Rather than a moment of discovery—Alexander Fleming noticing that a mold seemed lethal to bacteria or Archimedes leaping from his bath yelling, "Eureka!"—we should expect a more gradual process of knowledge gathering. Instead of one paradigm-defining discovery, coming to understand mental disorders will probably be much more like a team of paleontologists slowly brushing away dirt to reveal a set of fossils and developing ideas about how all the bones fit together to form a complete dinosaur.

Instead of a single theory—the X theory of depression—we will likely need multiple explanations that each focus on different mechanisms in the network. As hypothetical examples, theories might emerge at a neurological level showing how difficulty experiencing pleasure relates to difficulty sleeping, and at a psychological and ecological level explaining how changes that depressed people make to their environments contribute to the perpetuation of their mood (the latter example is inspired by this paper).

In the paper this essay is loosely based on, which will be published in the journal *Theory & Psychology*, my Ph.D. supervisor and I propose a structure to help researchers organize the process of discovery. We call it relational analysis of phenomena, or RAP. In RAP, researchers break down disorders into meaningful parts and richly describe these parts at multiple scales of analysis: What is going on in people's brains and bodies? How does it feel? What do they do? How does it change their environment? How do others react to it?

Only after this rigorous description process does the investigator try to explain the relationship between some of the parts. The overarching intention is to slowly uncover the mechanisms of the disorder in people's lives. Once we understand enough of the causes at play, we may begin to understand how the dysfunctional pattern of behavior is maintained and how best to effect positive change.

Ultimately some mental disorders might turn out to be like general paresis, with one well-defined cause in the brain. Others might turn out to be distortions in thought, behavior, and emotion supported by a network of mechanisms. Most disorders are probably somewhere in the middle, with one or more dominant causes and a plethora of less dominant ones. Because we don't really know, investing in multiple explanatory strategies seems the optimal way forward. The alternative—assuming that mental disorders are all brain disorders—places all our eggs in one basket.

We must develop effective treatments for mental disorders as rapidly as possible. But to do so we first need to be able to explain what is going on. Assuming from the get-go that brain dysfunction is always the cause is like shooting ourselves in the foot before we even start the race.

This article was published in Scientific American's *former blog network and reflects the views of the author, not necessarily those of* Scientific American.

About the Author

Kristopher Nielsen is a PhD student in the Explanation of Psychopathology and Crime lab at Victoria University of Wellington in New Zealand / Te Whare Wananga o te Upoko o te Ika a Maui.

Section 3: Habits for a Healthy Mind

Suppressing an Onrush of Toxic Thoughts Might Improve Your Mental Health

By Ingrid Wickelgren

Zulkayda Mamat is no stranger to traumatic memories. Ethnically Uighur, Mamat left China at age 12 after an uprising in the region of East Turkestan, where most of Mamat's extended family still lives. More than one million Uighurs have been arbitrarily detained in "political education" camps and prisons. "I know people in camps. I have witnessed families completely broken down, people in the diaspora, their entire lives changed," says Mamat, who just received her doctorate in cognitive neuroscience from the University of Cambridge.

Over the years, Mamat has noticed how the most resilient Uighurs she knows manage to cope with their trauma. Their formula is simple: they push the distressing memories out of their mind. Mamat herself is good at this. "It's almost intuitive to be able to control my thoughts," she says.

Clinical psychologists often warn against suppressing thoughts because they believe distressing ideas and images will bubble up later with greater frequency and worsen mental health problems. Psychoanalysis focuses on the contrasting approach of hunting down and exploring the meaning of any thoughts a person might have pushed to the back of their mind.

But Mamat now has data to support her intuition that suppression is beneficial. In a September 20 paper in *Science Advances,* she and her adviser, cognitive neuroscientist Michael Anderson, report that they successfully trained people—many of whom had mental health problems—to suppress their fears and that doing so improved these individuals' mental health. "Suppressing negative thoughts, far from being a hazardous thing to do," Anderson says, "actually seemed to be of great benefit, especially to the people who need it the most—people suffering from depression, anxiety, and post-traumatic stress."

92

The work also calls into question whether people with mental health disorders have an inherent inability to suppress intrusive thoughts. "It's probably not a deficit," Mamat says. The vast majority of people in the study, she says, "were surprised to see that this was something they could learn."

The technique bears a likeness to behavioral therapies in which people expose themselves to cues or situations that trigger fear and anxiety—heights, dirt, or parties, say—until the brain learns to inhibit those fear responses, says Charan Ranganath, a cognitive neuroscientist at the University of California, Davis, who was not involved in the research. But learning to halt the thoughts that arise from those cues is a novel approach. "What's surprising to me is telling people to stop that thought in and of itself is effective," Ranganath says. "That's an idea that could be really useful to bring into therapies."

Not everyone agrees that the approach is safe or likely to be successful as a therapeutic tool. But if further research suggests it is, suppression training might either be used alone or in conjunction with, say, cognitive-behavioral or exposure therapy, Anderson suggests.

The new findings stand in stark contrast to the conventional wisdom that thought suppression is both ineffective and harmful as a therapeutic approach. In the 1980s psychologist Daniel Wegner popularized this idea with his "white bear" experiments. In these studies, people were instructed not to think about a white bear. And in following those instructions, they later thought about white bears more often than did participants in a control group who had been initially told to think about the animals. Trying not to think about something, Wegner concluded, causes those same thoughts to pop up more often.

The idea has been influential in clinical psychology. Anderson and his colleagues, however, have generated data spanning two decades that suggest that pushing away negative memories causes those memories to fade and become less distressing. His experiments are meant to mimic a real-world scenario in which people encounter reminders of worrying thoughts and then need to decide whether to stem those thoughts or dwell on them.

Previously Anderson had not directly tested whether his technique, which he calls retrieval suppression, could be useful as a therapy. One potential problem was that the people with mental health conditions, who could benefit most from such a therapy, might be incapable of practicing it because of the way their brain functioned. Some data supported that idea, but Mamat was not convinced it was true. She thought anyone might be able to learn to stem their thoughts if they were shown how.

In March 2020 she decided to find out. COVID had halted all in-person research, including the brain-imaging project Mamat had been pursuing. It had also spawned a wave of anxiety, depression, and other mental health problems that needed to be addressed. Mamat told Anderson she wanted to test a therapy involving suppression that she could administer online from her apartment.

She cast a wide net for participants. English-speaking adults could volunteer as long as they were not color blind and did not have a neurological disorder or reading disability—and many of the volunteers did have mental health problems. Of the 120 people from 16 countries who participated in the study, 43 percent had clinically concerning levels of anxiety, 18 percent had significant depressive symptoms, and 24 percent had probable post-traumatic stress disorder (PTSD).

Before the training, Mamat asked each person to generate thoughts on which to base a set of cue words: 20 specific worries and fears that repeatedly intruded on their thoughts, 36 neutral events and 20 wishes for the future. As part of the study, the researchers took assessments of the participants' anxiety, depression, worry, and well-being.

Over three days, 61 of the participants were exposed to the cue words that represented their fears. For example, if someone was afraid that their parents would be hospitalized with COVID, the cue word might be "hospital." During training, they were instructed to stare at the reminder for several seconds and acknowledge the event but then to shut down all thoughts about it, as well as any associated imagery. If thoughts, feelings, or images did spring to mind, participants were to immediately push those ideas out of awareness and return their attention to the reminder. They were not to generate distracting thoughts because the researchers did not want any type of avoidance to be part of the strategy. A control group of 59 people were instructed to do the same for neutral events such as being seen by an optician.

In other trials, participants were told to conjure imagery to embellish and elaborate either neutral or positive events. The two groups suppressed each fear or neutral event or imagined each hope or neutral event 12 times each day for three days and were then tested on both the vividness and emotional impact of their thoughts.

As expected, suppression diminished the vividness and intensity of the fears. As a group, participants recalled details of their personal fears or neutral events less often and experienced reduced anxiety related to those fears.

More notably, suppressing fears improved people's mental health and did so much more than suppressing neutral scenarios. Worry, depression, and anxiety were all significantly reduced, and well-being increased. "What the training seems to be doing is giving people a way to stop from going into this vortex of worry when a negative thought comes up," Ranganath says. Surprisingly, imagining positive events produced no mental health benefits, suggesting that generating positive thoughts has far less power than blocking negative thoughts, Anderson says.

The researchers also showed that suppression did not lead memories to rebound, as the white bear experiments might suggest. Although there were individuals whose anxiety or depression worsened after training, there were fewer such cases in the group suppressing thoughts of feared events than among individuals who were blocking out neutral events. The researchers "went above and beyond" to demonstrate that the therapy did not have adverse effects, Ranganath says.

Three months after the training, depression scores continued to decline for the group as a whole. On measures of anxiety, worry, and PTSD, however, the effects of the training were only apparent among the people who had been depressed or anxious or showed signs of PTSD at the start of the study. "The people who were suffering at the outset showed a consistent benefit," Anderson says.

It appears that the more symptomatic a person had been, the more likely they were to use suppression after training, apparently because they found it useful. (No one was told to practice the technique after the three-day training period.) Among those with probable PTSD, for example, 82 percent reported reduced anxiety, and 63 percent said their mood improved—changes they attributed to suppression. "It's the people who were suffering at the outset who saw how much suppression benefited them," Anderson says.

Participants also reported that the training improved their ability to suppress thoughts; they rated their skill on the third day as much higher than they did on the first. Three quarters of the participants described being surprised or very surprised by their newfound faculty. "I couldn't believe how effective it was, and it made me realize how powerful my brain can be," one participant wrote.

The strategy has also drawn criticism, however. "[The paper] may lead some people to conclude that they should practice suppressing memories of a recent traumatic event, which, research suggests, may actually increase their risk of developing post-traumatic stress disorder," says Amanda Draheim, a psychologist at Goucher College in Baltimore.

Fully vetting the technique requires a randomized controlled clinical trial with several hundred participants, something Anderson has in his sights. Mamat has developed a phone app that could be used in such a trial, and she hopes it will eventually be available for widespread use.

During her study, Mamat got to know the participants, talking to them for hours from her apartment over Zoom. One of them broke down in tears and told Mamat that the experience had changed her life. Another described suppression as a "power" and planned to teach it to her children. The personal feedback convinced Mamat that the experiment was worthwhile, no matter what the data showed. "That was enough for me to have done this entire thing," she says. "That was beautiful. That was really beautiful."

About the Author

Ingrid Wickelgren is a freelance science journalist based in New Jersey.

Why Social Media Makes People Unhappy—And Simple Ways to Fix It

By Daisy Yuhas

D isrupted sleep, lower life satisfaction, and poor self-esteem are just a few of the negative mental health consequences that researchers have linked to social media. Somehow the same platforms that can help people feel more connected and knowledgeable also contribute to loneliness and disinformation. What succeeds and fails, scientists say, is a function of how these platforms are designed. Amanda Baughan, a graduate student specializing in human-computer interaction at the University of Washington, studies how social media triggers what psychologists call dissociation, or a state of reduced self-reflection and narrowed attention. She presented results at the 2022 Association for Computing Machinery Computer-Human Interaction Conference on Human Factors in Computing Systems. Baughan spoke with Mind Matters editor Daisy Yuhas to explain how and why apps need to change to give the people who use them greater power.

[An edited transcript of the interview follows.]

Q: You've shown how changing social media cues and presentations could improve well-being, even when people strongly disagree on issues. Can you give an example?

A: The design of social media can have a lot of power in how people interact with one another and how they feel about their online experiences. For example, we've found that social media design can actually help people feel more supportive and kind in moments of online conflict, provided there's a little bit of a nudge to behave that way. In one study, we designed an intervention that encouraged people who start talking about something contentious in a comment thread to switch to direct messaging. People really liked it. It helped to resolve their conflict and replicated a solution we use in-person: people having a public argument move to a private space to work things out.

Q: You've also tackled a different problem coming out of social media usage called the 30-Minute Ick Factor. What is that?

A: We very quickly lose ourselves on social media. When people encounter a platform where they can infinitely scroll for more information, it can trigger a similar neurocognitive reward system as in anticipating a winning lottery ticket or getting food. It's a powerful way that these apps are designed to keep us checking and scrolling.

The 30-Minute Ick Factor is when people mean to check their social media briefly but then find that 30 minutes have passed, and when they realize how much time they have spent, they have this sense of disgust and disappointment in themselves. Research has shown that people are dissatisfied with this habitual social media use. A lot of people frame it as meaningless, unproductive, or addictive.

Q: You've argued this experience is less a matter of addiction and more an issue of dissociation. Why?

A: Dissociation is a psychological process that comes in many forms. In the most common, everyday dissociation, your mind is so absorbed that you are disconnected from your actions. You could be doing the dishes, start daydreaming, and not pay attention to how you are doing the dishes. Or you might seek immersive experiences—watching a movie, reading a book, or playing a game—that pass the time and cause you to forget where you are.

During these activities, your sense of reflective self-consciousness and the passage of time is reduced. People only realize that they dissociated in hindsight. Attention is restored with the sense of "What just happened?" or "My leg fell asleep while we were watching that movie!"

Dissociation can be a positive thing, especially if it's an absorbing experience, meaningful activity, or a needed break.

But it can also be harmful in certain cases, as in gambling, or come in conflict with people's time-management goals, as with social media scrolling.

Q: How do you measure people's dissociation on social media?

A: We worked with 43 participants who used a custom mobile app that we created called Chirp to access their Twitter accounts. The app let people interact with Twitter content while allowing us to ask them questions and test interventions. So when people were using Chirp, after a given number of minutes, we would send them a questionnaire based on a psychological scale for measuring dissociation. We asked how much they agreed with the statement "I am currently using Chirp without really paying attention to what I'm doing" on a scale of 1 to 5. We also did interviews with 11 people to learn more. The results showed dissociation occurred in 42 percent of our participants, and they regularly reported losing track of time or feeling "all-consumed."

Q: You designed four interventions that modified people's Twitter experience on Chirp to reduce dissociation. What worked?

A: The most successful were custom lists and reading history labels. In custom lists, we forced users to categorize the content they followed, such as "sports" or "news" or "friends." Then, instead of interacting with Twitter's main feed, they engaged only with content on these lists. This approach was coupled with a reading history intervention in which people received a message when they were caught up on the newest tweets. Rather than continuing to scroll, they were alerted to what they had already seen, and so they focused on just the newest content. Those interventions reduced dissociation, and when we did interviews, people said they felt safer checking their social media accounts when these modifications were present.

In another design, people received timed messages letting them know how long they had been on Chirp and suggesting they leave. They also had the option of viewing a usage page that showed them statistics such as how much time they'd spent on Chirp in the past seven days. These two solutions were effective if people opted to use them. Many people ignored them, however. Also, they thought the timed messages were annoying. Those findings are interesting because a lot of the popular time-management tools available to people look like these time-out and usage notifications.

Q: So what could social media companies be doing differently? And is there any incentive for them to change?

A: Right now there is a lot working against people who use social media. It's impossible to ever fully catch up on a social media feed, especially when you consider the algorithmically inserted content such as Twitter's trending tweets or TikTok's "For You" page. But I think that there is hope that relatively simple tweaks to social media design, such as custom lists, can make a difference. It's important to note that the custom lists significantly reduced dissociation for people—but they did *not* significantly affect time spent using the app. To me, that points out that reducing people's dissociation may not be as antithetical to social media companies' revenue goals as we might intuitively think.

Q: What's most important for people using social media now to know?

A: First, don't pile a bunch of shame onto your social media habits. Thousands of people are employed to make you swipe your thumb up on that screen and keep you doing what you're doing. Let's shift the responsibility of designing safe and fulfilling experiences from users to the companies.

Second, get familiar with the well-being tools that are already offered. TikTok has a feature that, every hour, will tell you that you've been scrolling for a while and should consider a break. On Twitter, custom lists are a feature that already exists; it's just not the default option. If more people start using these tools, it could convince these companies to refine them.

Most important, vote for people who are interested in regulating technology because I think that's where we're going to see the biggest changes made.

About the Author

Daisy Yuhas edits the Scientific American *column Mind Matters. She is a freelance science journalist and editor based in Austin, Tex. Follow Yuhas on X (formerly Twitter) @DaisyYuhas.*

How Long Does It Really Take to Form a Habit?

By Jocelyn Solis-Moreira

Waking up at the crack of dawn and going for a run might feel intimidating when you start trying to make it a habit. Weaving a significant new activity such as this into your regular routine obviously takes determination and time—but how *much* time is really needed to make that habit stick?

One popular idea suggests that it takes 21 days to solidify a habit. A three-week time frame might sound easily reachable to someone making a resolution on New Year's Day, when people tend to feel extra motivated to start a new habit or kick an old one, says Colin Camerer, a behavioral economist at the California Institute of Technology who has conducted research on habit formation. Yet every January 21 very few people can boast that they have kept their resolutions. One survey showed that only 9 percent of people actually stuck to their goals in 2023.

Everyone has a unique habit-building timeline—and no matter how long it is for any individual, repetition is the key to making it work, explains Phillippa Lally, a senior lecturer in psychology and the co-director of the Habit Application and Theory group at the University of Surrey in England. Both Lally and Camerer suggest various individualized ways to reinforce healthy behaviors and to eventually turn a wholesome task into an unconscious habit.

Habit Formation Can Range from a Few Weeks to a Couple of Months

The origin of the "three-week theory" has nothing to do with habits, per se. It apparently originated from the 1960 self-help book *Psycho-Cybernetics*, in which plastic surgeon Maxwell Maltz observed that it took his patients about 21 days to get used to their new appearance after surgery. No formal experiment was conducted to verify this, but the book applied this 21-day timeline to self-transformation in many other wide-ranging aspects of life. For instance, the book also set three weeks as the time needed for people to get used to a new house or change their mind about their beliefs.

Even without much solid research, the 21-day myth became widely accepted. It likely persisted because it seems like such a reasonable amount of time, Camerer explains. Establishing a regular exercise habit in just three days feels seems too quick and implausible, for example, and a year seems too long and daunting. Camerer says people might easily see 21 days as a realistic and achievable time frame.

Almost a half century later, researchers finally gathered strong evidence that countered this idea. A hallmark 2009 study on habit creation found that habits developed in a range of 18 to 254 days; participants reported taking an average of about 66 days to reliably incorporate one of three new daily activities—eating a piece of fruit with lunch, drinking a bottle of water with lunch, or running for 15 minutes before dinner. Consistent daily repetition was the biggest factor influencing whether a behavior would become part of an automatic daily routine, says Lally, who was the first author on the study.

The type of activity is also a factor. Teaching yourself a completely new skill or process obviously takes longer than remembering to drink more water in the morning, Lally notes. A 2015 study found that new gym-goers had to exercise at least four times a week for six weeks in order to develop an exercise habit. And last year Camerer and his colleagues conducted a study that used machine learning to determine the time needed for habit-building. In it, machine-learning models analyzed vast amounts of data on repeated observations of a behavior and factored in different variables that may influence a person's decision to continue the behavior. The results showed that creating a handwashing habit took a few weeks, compared with the half year it took for people to develop an exercise habit. Handwashing, the study noted, is less complex than exercising and offers more opportunities to practice. The researchers also suggested that habit formation depends on the effort that a person puts into practicing an activity and on the presence of environmental cues that would remind them to carry out the behavior.

How to Maintain Consistency When Forming Good Habits

When it comes to keeping a resolution, Camerer notes it can be hard to stay motivated once the initial excitement of a "new year, new me" wears off. This can easily lead to lapsing or even dropping the activity completely after a couple of weeks. Creating a specific plan to perform the activity (for example, "study Spanish grammar for 20 minutes three times a week" versus the vague goal "learn more Spanish") and having some type of accountability (an app tracker or a friend) can help monitor progress and push a person to keep going. Additionally, people are more inclined to keep a resolution that they are interested in doing, rather than one that they simply believe they *should* do.

Rewards are great motivators but only when they're given right away. Lally says that people often make the mistake of delaying gratification—for example, by treating themselves to a shopping trip on Saturday after going to the gym all week. A reward is far more effective if received *during* the task. For instance, a person with an exercise goal could watch a newly released movie while running on the treadmill instead of waiting until the end of the week. Researchers in 2014 had people listen to then popular audiobooks (such as the *Hunger Games* trilogy and *The Devil Wears Prada*) that could only be accessed at the gym during the experiment and found that the participants initially went 51 percent more frequently than the control group.

Another tip Lally recommends is pairing the desired behavior with a reliable cue. For example, if a person goes to the office two days a week, scheduling gym sessions right after work reinforces an association that trains the brain. The more you relate the two behaviors, the stronger the resulting neural connections in brain regions involved in memory and habit formation.

Reconfiguring your physical space may also help. If your goal is to eat more fruit, for instance, Lally says you are more likely to do it if you keep a variety of fruits stocked and on display in your house. This also applies to breaking habits. People partaking in "Dry January" may empty the liquor cabinet beforehand to avoid temptation. While this might help temporarily, drug and alcohol addictions require more serious medical intervention and time.

What Happens If You Miss a Day?

Sometimes life happens; it is completely normal to miss a day or two in any new routine. Lally says that people tend to create rigid schedules that require carrying out a desired behavior every day—even when that's not really feasible. When people cannot meet their own expectations or if the activity itself (such as running 10 miles every day) is too hard, they can be deterred from trying again.

If you feel that you are falling off track, Lally advises taking a beat to evaluate why you are missing days and to come up with ways to fix the problem. Instead of running 10 miles every day, try jogging two miles three times a week. If that's still too challenging, adjust even more by slowing the pace or shortening the distance, and then eventually work yourself back up to the original goal. Putting on sneakers and walking down the block may not seem like much of an achievement at first, but it's a step in the right direction.

So don't kick yourself if you didn't reach your goal by the 21st of this month. As long as you keep at an activity, you *will* get better at it—no matter how long it takes.

About the Author

Jocelyn Solis-Moreira is a freelance journalist covering health and science. She is based in New York State.

The Nature Cure

By Jason G. Goldman

B y now it's almost common knowledge that spending time in nature is good for you. Areas with more trees tend to be less polluted, so spending time there allows you to breathe easier. Spending time outdoors has been linked with reduced blood pressure and stress and seems to motivate people to exercise more.

"So it'll come as no surprise that there's research showing that spending time in nature is good," says University of Exeter Medical School researcher Mathew P. White. "I mean, that's been known for millennia. There's dozens of papers showing that."

"We get this idea, patients are coming to us and they're saying, 'doctor, how long should I spend?' and the doctor is saying, 'I don't really know.'"

So White and his team decided to find out by using data collected from nearly 20,000 people in England through the Monitor of Engagement with the Natural Environment Survey.

And their answer? Two hours a week. People who spent at least that much time amid nature—either all at once or totaled over several shorter visits—were more likely to report good health and psychological well-being than those with no nature exposure.

Remarkably, the researchers found that less than two hours offered no significant benefits. So what's so special about two hours?

"I have absolutely no idea. Really. We didn't have an a priori guess at what this would be, this threshold. It emerged. And I'd be lying if I said we predicted this. I don't know."

Even more noteworthy, the two-hour benchmark applied to men and women, to older and younger folks, to people from different ethnic backgrounds, occupational groups, socioeconomic levels, and so on. Even people with long-term illnesses or disabilities benefited from time spent in nature—as long as it was at least 120 minutes per week. The study is in the journal *Scientific Reports*.

While the findings are based on a tremendous number of people, White cautions that it's really just a correlation. Nobody knows why or how nature has this benefit or even if the findings will stand up to more rigorous investigation.

"I want to be really clear about this. This is very early stages. We're not saying everybody has to do 120. This is really to start the conversation, saying, what would a threshold look like? What research do we need to take this to the next step before doctors can have the true confidence to work with their patients? But it's certainly a starting point."

About the Author

Jason G. Goldman is a science journalist based in Los Angeles. He has written about animal behavior, wildlife biology, conservation, and ecology for Scientific American, Los Angeles *magazine, the* Washington Post, *the* Guardian, *the BBC,* Conservation *magazine, and elsewhere. He contributes to* Scientific American's *"60-Second Science" podcast, and is co-editor of* Science Blogging: The Essential Guide *(Yale University Press). He enjoys sharing his wildlife knowledge on television and on the radio, and often speaks to the public about wildlife and science communication.*

The Way to Well-Being

By Andrea Gawrylewski

Every new year millions of people vow to finally get it together and improve themselves—from health factors, to relationships, to overall happiness in life. Yet statistics show that fewer than half of them will have stuck to their resolutions even six months later. Are humans so weak-willed? Or are our tactics of self-improvement flawed?

To be sure, self-improvement requires effort and discipline, and the latest diet and lifestyle crazes are often cocktails of unsubstantiated claims and promises. Yet science has identified a variety of methods that can help us to live better lives. In this special issue, we explain what the latest research has discovered about attaining professional success, finding contentment in life, and increasing physical and emotional wellness.

Considering that five days a week most of us spend more than 50 percent of our waking hours at work, the occupational environment can be a great place to start. Beat stress using a 10-pronged approach that includes building a support network and reinterpreting negative events. Cultivate creative thinking by breaking your normal routines and habits. Also, increase your overall performance by completely disconnecting from work on a regular basis.

At work and beyond, learning to control your emotions can lead to a calmer, more balanced existence. On the home front, focusing on positive experiences with your partner can enhance the joy in your relationship. To boost your mood, try out a 10- to 15-minute meditation to improve your focus and attention. And if you need a creative spark, try opening your mind by engaging in novel pursuits. You will look at the world in a whole new light.

One of the simplest ways to power up? Get moving! Beyond burning calories, consistent cardio and weight routines charge the immune, endocrine, and neurological systems. In fact, a large health trial recently reported that regular workouts can stave off dementia, even in people older than 60. In addition to exercising, don't forget to eat well: the right diet is good for both body and mind.

Finally, whatever the year brings, remember to take it easy. Mounting evidence is showing that adopting a policy of self-compassion reduces stress and bolsters resilience, whether or not you achieve your goals. So give yourself a break and handle your own heart with care. It might be the ticket to happier living.

About the Author

Andrea Gawrylewski is chief newsletter editor at Scientific American. *She writes the daily* Today in Science *newsletter and oversees all other newsletters at the magazine. In addition, she manages all special collector's editions and in the past was the editor for* Scientific American Mind, Scientific American Space & Physics *and* Scientific American Health & Medicine. *Gawrylewski got her start in journalism at the* Scientist *magazine, where she was a features writer and editor for "hot" research papers in the life sciences. She spent more than six years in educational publishing, editing books for higher education in biology, environmental science and nutrition. She holds a master's degree in earth science and a master's degree in journalism, both from Columbia University, home of the Pulitzer Prize.*

You Can't Fix Burnout With Self-Care

By Shayla Love and Timmy Broderick

Anthony Montgomery: The most important part of burnout is that it's about yourself, but it's also about others.

[CLIP: Opening music]

Shayla Love: One of my New Year's resolutions was to be less burned-out. Maybe you can relate; you think, 'I'm going to better manage my stress this year. I'm going to make time for activities that I find nourishing and finally nail that work/life balance.' But just a few weeks into January, I found myself hitting a wall. The sense of renewal of a new year didn't manifest. The burnout I felt from 2023 had followed me—all the way into February.

Burnout feels like something that descends upon you and then is impossible to shake off. A 2021 study found that around three in five employees felt symptoms of burnout, and COVID didn't make it easier. More people found their work lives getting more unmanageable during the pandemic, not less. When my resolution to fix my burnout with effort didn't work, I wanted to go back to the beginning of burnout's story and understand what it is.

I'm Shayla Love, and you're listening to *Scientific American*'s Science, Quickly.

Today we're revisiting the concept of burnout: a word people use to describe how they feel exhausted, psychically tired with their jobs—that they may love!—or drained by the other obligations in their never ending to-do lists.

Christina Maslach: I didn't start out with any particular interest or plan to study burnout, because I'd never heard about something like that.

Love: That's Christina Maslach, a professor emerita at the University of California, Berkeley, in the Interdisciplinary Center for Healthy Workplaces. I called her up because one of the main measurement tools for burnout is named after her: the Maslach Burnout Inventory, or MBI.

Maslach: This was in the early to mid-'70s.

Love: Her research was on how people manage strong emotions. She decided to interview people such as emergency room doctors or police officers, who dealt with intense work environments. When her conversations were coming to a close, people would often say:

Maslach: "Can I tell you something else? Can I talk to you about this other thing?"

Love: People shared that they were stressed, exhausted, and feeling disconnected. Christina didn't have a name for it, but one day, she met a woman who worked in poverty law. The woman said that in her world, this was called burnout. Christina brought this term to her subjects, and the response was immediate.

Maslach: "How about burnout?" "Yes! that's it!" You know, it would be such an immediate reaction.

Love: Around the same time, a psychologist named Herbert Freudenberger published a paper in 1974 about how he and some colleagues working in a free clinic started to respond to the workload and stresses. People were starting "to fail, wear out, or become exhausted by making excessive demands on energy, strength, or resources," he wrote, and it was happening to the most dedicated and committed people he knew. Christina continued to gather stories from people who felt the same way. When her first article came out about burnout in a popular science magazine called *Human Behavior*...

Maslach: That article went, in today's terms, viral. People were calling me; I was getting sacks full of mail, you know, snail mail, from people saying, "Oh, my God, I just read it; I thought I was the only one."

Love: Burnout has clearly resonated for a long time. Hearing these older stories reminded me of the overwhelming response to writer Anne Helen Petersen's 2019 article on millennial burnout in *BuzzFeed News*. So many people I knew shared that article back and forth, asking each other: Do you feel this way too?

[CLIP: Anne Helen Petersen: "I kind of went numb."]

Love: This is Anne describing how she felt to the psychologist Adam Grant.

[CLIP: Anne Helen Petersen: "I didn't feel like anything was exciting that I wanted to cover. I didn't feel like I had any good ideas. I cried on Skype with my editor, which is very out of character for me."]

Love: So what is this feeling that's been haunting us for decades?

Anthony Montgomery: I've been working on burnout for the last 20 years.

Love: Anthony Montgomery is a professor of occupational and organizational psychology at Northumbria University in England. I asked him what we've learned about how burnout feels since the '70s, when Christina and others first started circling around it.

Montgomery: The first part is you feel overwhelmed and exhausted. The second part is you have heightened feelings of cynicism and detach from the job.

Love: These play into the third quality, which is a sense of ineffectiveness.

Montgomery: You feel like you're not accomplishing your work.

Love: Burnout is not a medical diagnosis, though there's overlap between burnout and conditions such as depression or anxiety. It's a response to chronic conditions in which you are overworked and don't feel like you're making a difference or progressing. But here's maybe the most important part that's come out over the years: these feelings don't come from you alone.

Montgomery: The most important component of burnout is not to keep it at the individual level.

Love: Burnout arises from your interaction with your circumstances and the environment. This is why individual interventions for burnout don't really work. The solution to burnout is not, as I tried, to make a personal resolution about it. It's actually to look outward and ask: Why am I experiencing this? What about my job or interactions is leading to this feeling?

Montgomery: Burnout as a concept means that there's something about the way your work is organized, which is causing you burnout or which is, you know, provoking burnout in yourself. So in a sense, the most important thing to do is for us to ask, you know, what is it about the way my work is arranged that is influencing the degree to which I feel burned-out?

Love: Honestly, this made me feel both better and worse. It finally made sense why I couldn't self-care my way out of burnout, but this was also disempowering. If my burnout comes from my interaction with the outside world, and I can't fix the world, will I be burned-out forever?

Amelia Nagoski: *Burnout* is the book that I needed.

Love: That's Amelia Nagoski. She wrote *Burnout: The Secret to Unlocking the Stress Cycle* with her sister Emily in 2018. She was getting her Doctorate of Musical Arts in conducting and...

Nagoski: I ended up in the hospital twice with stress-induced illness. My sister, being Emily Nagoski, Ph.D., *New York Times* bestselling author, brought me stacks of peer reviewed science because, you know, that's the love language in our families: peer review.

Love: Amelia tells me that at the same time as we recognize that burnout comes from our interactions with difficult outward environments, we still have power to feel better inwardly.

Nagoski: Even though the things that are causing our stress are sometimes beyond our control, the stress that's happening is a cycle that happens in our body.

Love: Their book is focused on how to complete an emotion cycle instead of getting stuck in the middle of feeling stressed and having it drag on in perpetuity.

Nagoski: We can deal with that stress that's happening in our body in a separate process than the process we use to deal with the things that cause our stress.

Love: This is where "self-care" comes into play: things such as exercise, breathing, and spending time with friends. But these interventions aren't to fix the stressors that cause burnout—those are social. They're to help you get out of fight-or-flight mode.

Montgomery: It's the fact that it's a social thing in your work means you can do something about it, you know, a lot of time. You know, your boss or your line manager might say, well, listen, we can't give you more money; we can't give you more time off. And sometimes they can't. And these things are difficult. But what they can do is they can work with you and your colleagues to change the way you work in a way that makes you feel less stress, less burnout.

Love: It's interesting to me that burnout research is entirely focused on work, and yet there has been what *The Atlantic*'s Olga Khazan and others have called "burnout creep," which is using the word burnout in situations that extend beyond our jobs—parenting burnout, volunteering burnout, being burned-out on your favorite food. We're using it as a synonym for anything that we've lost joy in.

Do you think that maybe a lot of people feel mentally exhausted and they want to understand why that is or have a word for it?

Montgomery: I think it's become very popular, but it can be quite useful as well. So, I mean, we don't need to get into a sort of very unhelpful academic debate where, you know, are you, do you have all the symptoms of burnout. I think what's important at a practical level, you know—how, you know, how can a person tell if they're burned-out? What can they do about it?

Love: After thinking about it, I've decided that as far as frameworks go for understanding our frustrations, exhaustion and malaise, I can think of worse ones. And that's because burnout, as it was originally conceived, is a social problem. It's not that you are tired of parenting or volunteering for no reason. It's probably because you're not getting enough help, you don't feel like you're making an impact and you're not in control of your schedule or what you're doing. You can't take on the job of feeling better all by yourself. We need help, and we need to help each other.

Montgomery: It rarely happens just to one person. If you're feeling burnt out, it's quite likely the people around you, people who you work with, are having similar feelings as well.

Love: For Science, Quickly, this is Shayla Love.

Science, Quickly is produced by Tulika Bose and Jeff DelViscio and edited by Timmy Broderick, Alexa Feder and Alexa Lim. Music is by Dominic Smith. Subscribe to Science, Quickly for updated and in-depth science news.

[The above is a transcript of this podcast.]

About the Author

Shayla Love is a journalist based in Brooklyn, N.Y. She writes about science, health and the intersection of history, culture and philosophy with present-day research. Follow Love on X (formerly Twitter) @shayla__love.

Section 4: Advancements in Mental Health Research and Treatment

Funding for Research on Psychedelics Is on the Rise, Along with Scientists' Hopes for Using Them

By Rachel Nuwer

Gül Dölen: I remember when I first applied to the NIH, my program officer was like, "No, nobody will ever give psychedelics as a therapy. You're barking up the wrong tree. You should be studying why these things are bad for the brain."

Nuwer: This was back in 2014, when Johns Hopkins neuroscientist Gül Dölen was trying to get funding to study whether psychedelic drugs might be master keys for reopening critical periods in the brain.

Dölen: I was like, "No, I think this is a great idea, and if we're right about it, we're going to win the Nobel Prize. I want to get credit for having this idea right now and will not change my grant to accommodate your view." And so I was very stubborn, and I didn't get the grant, and I didn't get many, many, many other ones after that.

Nuwer: For Science, Quickly, I'm science journalist and author Rachel Nuwer. You're listening to part three of a three-part series on the science of psychedelics.

If Gül was submitting the same grant application today, she'd probably have a much stronger shot at getting it.

Dölen: There's definitely been a sea change in terms of the attitudes toward funding psychedelics.

Nuwer: As funding opportunities for psychedelic science increase, researchers are beginning to put serious thought into mind-bending studies that previously would have seemed like fantasy.

Gül, for example, is currently seeking funding for a study she's designed to see if psychedelics could be used to reopen a motor-learning critical period that would allow stroke patients to regain lost function.

Dölen: If it ends up being the case that psychedelics are able to do this, then it offers therapy for roughly 500,000 [or] 400,000 people a year in the United States alone who have a stroke but then don't recover full function.

Nuwer: I was curious about what other researchers are most excited about in the field, so I reached out to several other leading thinkers to see what kind of psychedelic investigations they're envisioning for the future.

Albert Garcia-Romeu is a research scientist at the Johns Hopkins University School of Medicine. He works mainly on using psychedelics in a clinical setting. Until now, studies of psychedelic-assisted therapy had mostly focused on post-traumatic stress disorder, depression, addiction, and end-of-life anxiety, but there could be all sorts of other applications.

Albert Garcia-Romeu: Now you're starting to see this multiply out into lots of different clinical areas, including things like anorexia nervosa. I'm doing a study [of] early-stage Alzheimer's disease.

I have a study under development for people with long COVID. There's lots of different directions to take the work, which is pretty neat, being a scientist, because it kind of makes you feel like you're a kid in a candy shop.

Nuwer: Albert is also interested in studying how psychedelics might affect well people—that is, people who don't have any particular disease but who just want to use the substances for things such as inner exploration, spirituality, personal enhancement, connection, or just having fun.

Garcia-Romeu: It's something that's been around as long as written history, and so it really makes us think, "How can these substances be used outside of the medical framework?"

Nuwer: Albert imagines a study, for example, in which psychedelics are given to people to see if the drugs could help enhance creativity. Surprisingly, there is a precedent for this. Back in the 1960s, researchers at Stanford University actually gave healthy people LSD and mescaline to test this question.

Garcia-Romeu: They were taking all these kind of educated professionals and having them come in and [saying], "Think about one of the challenging problems that you're facing in your work now.

Now we're going to go ahead and give you one of these drugs and see if that can help you to have some further insight or come up with some potential solutions for that."

It definitely yielded some really interesting and fruitful results where people did come out of that with things like patents and designs for new types of devices and, and buildings. And so ... that's something that I think is incredibly interesting, especially being at, you know, a place like Hopkins.

You can talk to physicists, astrophysicists, people who are doing all sorts of different work on cancer biology and really see, like, wow, there's a possibility here that we could take some of these people and put them through a protocol that would help them to think about the problems that they're working on from a different perspective. And that, in turn, may yield some really, really fascinating and innovative new ways of dealing with problems that we're now facing.

We're in an era right now of all of these different types of crises.

And so in the midst of all this, how can we also position psychedelics as allies or as tools that we can use to hopefully better navigate this rapidly changing and pretty chaotic era that we find ourselves in?

Nuwer: Psychedelics might also be used to help us get through difficult times by allowing researchers to dissect and better understand another very important component of the human experience: happiness.

Sonja Lyubomirsky: My name is Sonja Lyubomirsky, and I'm a professor of psychology at the University of California of Riverside. I've been studying happiness for almost 35 years.

My lab does what we call happiness intervention.

And we do randomized controlled trials. They're kind of like clinical trials, but instead of testing a new vaccine, we're testing, like, a happiness strategy, like gratitude or kindness.

Nuwer: After years of research, Sonja realized that strategies for making people feel happier tend to boil down to one key thing: making them feel more connected to other people.

Lyubomirsky: So I became interested in connection and "How do we foster connection?"

Nuwer: But this created a challenge for Sonja.

Lyubomirsky: It's really hard to study this in the lab: You know, how—how can you actually foster, like, sort of bottle that feeling of sort of deep connection with someone when you truly feel understood and loved?

Nuwer: In pondering how to go about studying this in the lab, it dawned on Sonja that the psychedelic drug MDMA could provide a perfect solution.

Lyubomirsky: It turns out that MDMA is a substance that can actually kind of provide a little shortcut for scientists.

There are really two ways that I see studying MDMA. One is how you can sort of use it to bottle this sense of connection and feeling understood and empathy, and then that enables you to study the psychological mechanisms and the brain pathways.

But the other way is: You could try to use it to improve people's lives, right? There's sort of this epidemic of loneliness we have. People are feeling disconnected.

Can we actually improve people's lives—and not just people who have mental health conditions but just people who are maybe a little bit lonely or people who want to improve their relationships?

Nuwer: In 2022 Sonja thought MDMA could be such a powerful investigative tool for psychologists and social scientists that she authored a paper proposing a new field called psychedelic social science.

She imagines future research using MDMA and other psychedelics to study everything from the fundamental components of positive relationships to whether it might be possible to shift someone's extremist views.

Lyubomirsky: I hope that there are young people in the field who want to kind of take the helm and lead it and develop it.

Nuwer: Psychedelics could eventually also help to answer fundamental questions about existence and who or what we really are.

David Presti: Deepening our understanding of the nature of mind and consciousness is among the most exciting frontiers of contemporary science, and there are so many mysteries there. And there's every reason to believe that whatever the psychedelic materials are tapping into when it comes to their impact on the brain, the nervous system, the body is interacting with the mind and our conscious awareness, and all the aspects of what mind may be, in a way that is radically different from anything else we've ever researched.

Nuwer: That's David Presti, a neurobiologist at the University of California, Berkeley. As psychedelics open up new frontiers of neuroscience, David says it's important for researchers to try to put aside their preexisting assumptions about what he calls 'the deep mysteries of the mind.'

Presti: I really think there's a capacity to contribute to taking our understanding of the relationship between mind and brain and body and physical reality writ large to a deeper level of insight if we are open to that.

Nuwer: David also encourages psychedelic scientists to strike up dialogues with experts in religion or spirituality.

Presti: At the core of many religious traditions, there is a kind of an appreciation for the deep mystery of reality and who we are within that deep mystery of reality. This is an incredibly important system of narratives that play out and have huge impact in human society all over the planet.

To begin to appreciate that within the context of biophysical science would be a really beautiful thing because there has been so much belief that has evolved over the last several hundred years of this disconnection between what we call science and what we call religion, and there's no reason that has to be the case.

Both science and religion deal with the deep mystery of reality and our place in it. And so I see this as really all one question that can provide a platform for much more engagement between religious narratives and scientific narratives.

Nuwer: David hopes that these kinds of collaborations seeded by psychedelics will also lead to practical results in terms of how humans treat each other, other species, and the planet.

Presti: Beginning to see how deeply interconnected and really sentient in some way—very different from ours but a kind of sentience, it's there—that may allow us a springboard for developing greater respect and greater thoughtfulness for how we interact with these sentient systems.

I can only hope so.

Nuwer: For Science, Quickly, I'm Rachel Nuwer. You've just listened to part three of a three-part series on the science of psychedelics.

Science, Quickly is produced by Tulika Bose, Jeff DelViscio, Kelso Harper, and Carin Leong and edited by Elah Feder and Alexa Lim. Don't forget to listen to Science, Quickly wherever you get your podcasts and visit ScientificAmerican.com for updated and in-depth science news.

[The above is a transcript of this podcast.]

About the Author

Rachel Nuwer is a freelance science journalist and author who regularly contributes to Scientific American, *the* New York Times *and* National Geographic, *among other publications. Follow Nuwer on X (formerly Twitter) @RachelNuwer.*

A Newly Discovered Brain Signal Marks Recovery from Depression

By Ingrid Wickelgren

O n February 4, 2019, before he was wheeled into the operating room, Tyler Hajjar, then age 28, hugged his mother and quipped, "It's just brain surgery." Hajjar, a resident of Johns Creek, Ga., had traveled to Emory University in Atlanta to outfit his brain with a device that might reset it in hopes of easing the depression that had severely diminished his quality of life—and, at times, threatened that life—for a decade. "Sometimes the best thing I could do was literally just lay in bed all day," he recalls of his long illness, "but honestly, that was better than anything else that was going through my mind—which would have been irreversible."

Hajjar wasn't afraid of the surgery itself—only that it wouldn't work. More than 20 medications, by his count, hadn't helped him in any durable way; neither had electroconvulsive therapy, transcranial magnetic stimulation (TMS), or ketamine infusions.

But there was reason for optimism. Since the first trials in the early 2000s, deep-brain stimulation (DBS), in the hands of expert teams such as the one at Emory, has led to lasting relief in dozens of people with treatment-resistant depression. The technique, which remains experimental for depression—it did not meet the threshold for success in two large randomized controlled clinical trials—involves effectively rebooting the brain using implanted electrodes that stimulate it with pulses of electricity.

Though Hajjar hoped for a clinical benefit, his surgery was designed to also help uncover something novel: a wellness signal from the brain. He and nine others received a device that not only delivered electricity to the brain but also sensed neural activity. Analyzing that activity and correlating it with clinical ratings yielded a biomarker that signaled when a person was better in an enduring way.

The results, reported on September 20 in *Nature*, reveal a neural code that represents the first known signal of the presence or absence of depression in the brain. "This is to me, studying depression for more than 30 years, the closest clue to know, fundamentally, 'What is depression, and how do we think about how the brain can be repaired?'" says Helen Mayberg, a neurologist at the Icahn School of Medicine at Mount Sinai, who was co-senior author of the study.

The new biomarker could improve the efficacy of the technology because it tells doctors when a person's symptoms call for an adjustment in the stimulation and when they don't—and, if tested further, it might even serve as a predictor of depression relapse. With such guidance, a larger number of doctors could capably care for people who have undergone DBS. "It could be very useful to bedside clinicians and to making the therapy more scalable, more effective and, frankly, helping the physician to do no harm," says Michael Okun, a neurologist at the University of Florida, who was not involved in the study. Okun is a co-founder of the DBS Think Tank, an annual forum centered on cutting-edge issues involving the technology. Nearly three million people in the U.S. have treatment-resistant depression and stand to benefit from an approved therapy.

The work also could spur advances in less invasive treatments that modulate brain activity, such as TMS (which involves placing a coil on the scalp to create a magnetic field), says Gordon Baltuch, a neurosurgeon at Columbia University Irving Medical Center, who did not participate in the new research. "Neuromodulation could potentially help a cohort of people who have a disease which is not only disabling but is fatal" to tens of thousands of people each year in the U.S., Baltuch says.

Other biomarkers for depression could follow if, say, changes in a person's face or voice, or in brain waves detected at the surface of the brain, correlate with the internal signal. Study investigators found a pattern of facial expressions that changed in tandem with the brain's state, which is a promising sign. "There are probably many ways we will be able to read out from the brain, invasively and noninvasively," says Christopher Rozell, a neuroengineer at

Georgia Institute of Technology, who identified the wellness signal and was co-senior author on the new study. "It opens the floodgates for people to be able to look for these sorts of signals."

The subcallosal cingulate, also known as "Brodmann area 25," is embedded deep in the brain, above and behind the eyes. It is a critical crossroads for four major nerve fiber tracts and thus an intersection of brain traffic coming from areas that control all the functions that go awry in depression—emotional regulation, sleep, appetite, reward, motivation, and memory, among others.

Two decades ago Mayberg was mapping brain circuits involved in depression and noticed that every time an antidepressant worked, area 25 became less active. So she decided to see if stimulating the brain there could modulate the area's activity and ease depression in the most intractable cases, where other treatments had failed. Over the course of 20 years, she and her teams found that it could. In a 2019 follow-up study on 28 people treated with DBS, for example, Mayberg and her colleagues reported that half or more of the individuals significantly improved, and about 30 percent achieved remission and stayed well two to eight years later. One patient of Mayberg's has stayed in remission for 18 years. "People just don't get better; they stay better," Mayberg says. Response rates have now climbed to about 80 percent as new techniques enable better targeting of area 25 in individual brains, Mayberg says.

Although Mayberg knew the treatment worked, at least in her patients, she did not know how. In 2013 Mayberg, then at Emory, heard about prototype stimulators made by the medical device company Medtronic that could also record from the brain, and she applied to receive 10 of them. She teamed up with Rozell and his colleagues, who had the skills to make sense of what the sensors were picking up.

In 2015 Emory neurosurgeons implanted the first of the new devices by threading one electrode into area 25 in each hemisphere and connecting these to a pacemaker. Each electrode has four contacts, places where it interfaces with brain tissue around area 25. Four years later Hajjar was the last member of this cohort to have the operation. In the operating room, he was awakened briefly, and he reported that stimulation of one of the contacts on the left side of the brain brought on a new feeling of emotional lightness—one that would, if he weren't bolted in, enable him to go out with his father to a shooting range to participate in an activity that they both enjoyed.

It was a promising sign. Over the course of six months, the device collected data from Hajjar's brain and picked up a constellation of brain waves that reflected the combined activity of thousands of neurons. "Like a symphony where you have some high-pitched instruments and some low-pitched instruments, we can take these brain signals and decompose them into frequencies in different ranges," Rozell says.

Hajjar and the others in the study also had a weekly clinical assessment, which was videotaped. Within a couple of months, most participants felt somewhat better. After six months, symptoms had diminished by at least half in nine of the 10 individuals, and seven achieved remission. Only six of them, however, had usable brain data, and five of the six showed the typical pattern of improvement.

Using data from those five people, Rozell and his team built artificial intelligence software to compare participants' brain wave patterns at the start of the study, when they were sick, with those patterns at the end, when they were better. The researchers found a coordinated change in a few frequency bands that could distinguish a sick brain from a brain that was well with 90 percent accuracy. "It's the very first time that we've really been able to get a brain readout of recovery," Rozell says.

The signal was the same for all the participants, but it showed up at different times: at eight weeks in one person and at 20 weeks in another, for example. When a doctor sees it, they know that regardless of their patient's current state of mind, they can leave the stimulation as is, says Patricio Riva-Posse, the study's lead psychiatrist. "There is an objective biomarker beyond my impression as a psychiatrist that can tell me, 'Oh yes, this patient is slowly getting better,'" Riva-Posse says. It can also provide people being treated reassurance that they are on the right path. "We have a goal line for recovery," Mayberg says.

The sixth participant with usable brain data showed an atypical trajectory after treatment. She felt better after the operation and stayed well for four months, but then she relapsed. The scientists looked for the wellness signal in her after the fact. She had it at the start of her treatment, but it disappeared a month before she relapsed—and so it could have served as a warning sign. "If we would have had it, we would have turned up [her stimulation] a month earlier. She might not have gotten into trouble," Mayberg says.

Using artificial intelligence software, the researchers also found changes in a person's face that paralleled the appearance of the brain's wellness signal. Those changes fell short of a clinically useful biomarker, Rozell says, because the study was too small to define a pattern that was both specific for depression and common to all participants. Still, the finding points to the possibility of a more universal indicator of recovery. "We will build models that aren't just for my small cohort of lucky patients but that could generalize to everybody," Mayberg says.

Brain scans might also offer clues to wellness. Scans of the study participants' brain before their surgery showed that the degree of damage to certain nerve fiber tracts correlated with the severity of their depression. The researchers could not look for a change in those tracts with the treatment, however, because the participants could not be put in a brain scanner once the implant was in place.

The latest DBS technology is compatible with brain imaging. A team at Mount Sinai has now implanted some of these new devices in another group of 10 participants and will look not only for the wellness biomarker but also for evidence of a repaired brain circuit, Mayberg says.

Formal approval of DBS for depression requires randomized controlled clinical trials. One earlier such trial targeting area 25 did not demonstrate a benefit over a sham procedure when its sponsor, St. Jude Medical (now Abbott), halted it in 2013 at the halfway point. Yet some people improved after the stopping point, and the accumulated results and lessons from small trials leave a lot of room for hope, experts say. (Another trial targeting a different place in the brain using a DBS system from Medtronic also had disappointing results.)

Despite these setbacks, the technology has not been abandoned as a depression treatment. "It's a multibillion-dollar industry. People are going to keep trying until they get it," Okun says. "They are getting closer, and the data is getting better and better as they see these groups improving their outcomes."

Abbott is gearing up for a do-over. In July 2022 the U.S. Food and Drug Administration granted the company a breakthrough device designation for the use of the company's DBS system in treatment-resistant depression, thereby expediting its development and, if all goes well, eventual approval. Abbott is now working with the FDA on a plan for a clinical trial, according to Jenn Wong, the company's divisional vice president of global clinical and regulatory affairs in their neuromodulation business.

At the six-month mark, Hajjar went into remission. He started hanging out with friends he hadn't seen in a while and was able to take on some temporary work. "I felt like I could get back into the world," he recalls. He still struggled with anxiety, however, and in 2021 his depression began to reemerge. But adjustments to the stimulation brought him back.

Hajjar is now employed part-time and has had several speaking gigs in which he has shared his story with surgeons, scientists, and medical students at conferences or over Zoom. He is even making tentative plans for the future—including pursuing his long-term interest in mechanical drafting. Perhaps most importantly, he has a new outlook on life. "I look forward to waking up in the morning," he says.

About the Author

Ingrid Wickelgren is a freelance science journalist based in New Jersey.

To Solve the LGBTQ Youth Mental Health Crisis, Our Research Must Be More Nuanced

By Myeshia Price

O ur youth are in a mental health crisis. Young people describe steadily increasing sadness, hopelessness, and suicidal thoughts. These mental health challenges are greater for youth who hold marginalized identities that include sexual orientation, gender identity, or race or ethnicity. Near-constant exposure to traumatizing media and news stories, such as when Black youth watch videos of people who look like them being killed or when transgender youth hear multiple politicians endorse and pass laws that deny their very existence, compounds these disparities.

But young people do not fall into neat categories of race, ethnicity, sexual orientation, or gender identity. They reject antiquated norms and societal expectations, especially around gender and sexuality. Yet most research on people in this group, especially on LGBTQ youth, does not fully account for how they identify themselves. Approaching research as though sex is binary and gender is exact leads to incomplete data. This mistake keeps us from creating the best possible mental health policies and programs.

We need to collect robust data on specific populations of LGBTQ young people to better understand the unique risks they face, such as immigration concerns that Latinx youth may have that others may not. We can also better understand factors that uphold well-being, such as how family support affects Black trans and nonbinary youth.

LGBTQ young people of color, including those who identify in more nuanced ways than either gay or lesbian, are more likely to struggle with their mental health than their white LGBTQ counterparts. As researchers, if we can equip ourselves with this information about their unique needs and experiences, we can create intervention strategies that support the mental health of every

LGBTQ young person rather than attempting to apply a "broad strokes" approach that assumes what works for one group must work for all.

As director of research science at the Trevor Project, the premier suicide prevention organization for LGBTQ youth, I lead projects that examine LGBTQ young people and their mental health in an intersectional way, accounting for the many facets of their identities and how society and culture influence how they value themselves. I and my colleagues conduct studies with groups of people who are geographically diverse and gender- and race-diverse to understand what drives mental health distress in a way that allows us to address specific needs in different populations. For advocates trying to improve mental health outcomes, this means they must consider stigma, how it turns into victimization, discrimination, and rejection and how it disproportionately affects people who hold multiple marginalized identities.

Our *2023 U.S. National Survey on the Mental Health of LGBTQ Young People*, for example, found that LGBTQ youth with multiple marginalized identities reported greater suicide risk, compared with their peers who did not have more than one marginalized identity. To learn this, we asked young people demographic questions about race/ethnicity, sexual orientation, and gender identity amid a battery of assessments. Based on survey questions about mental health and suicide risk, we've found that nearly one in five transgender or nonbinary young people (18 percent) attempted suicide in the past year, compared with nearly one in 10 cisgender young people whose sexual orientation was lesbian, gay, bisexual, queer, pansexual, asexual, or questioning (8 percent). Among almost all groups of LGBTQ young people of color, the rates of those who said they had attempted suicide—22 percent of Indigenous youth, 18 percent of Middle Eastern/Northern African youth, 16 percent of Black youth, 17 percent of multiracial youth, and 15 percent of Latinx youth—were higher than that of white LGBTQ youth (11 percent). And youth who identified as pansexual attempted suicide at a significantly higher rate than lesbian, gay, bisexual, queer, asexual, and questioning youth.

The majority of research exploring LGBTQ young people's mental health does not have the sample size to do subgroup analyses in this way or, in rare cases, opts to unnecessarily aggregate findings (such as when bisexual young people are not analyzed separately despite representing the majority of the LGBTQ population). Our recruitment goals are set on finding enough people in harder-to-reach groups, such as Black transgender and nonbinary young people, and not to simply have a high overall sample size. In doing so, we are able to analyze findings specific to each group and also ensure these findings reach a wide audience. However, just as other researchers, when we are unable to collect enough data for subgroups to appropriately power our analyses, we do not publish those findings.

What we hope is that people working in small community settings can design targeted prevention programs. For example, an organization that aims to improve well-being among Latinx LGBTQ young people can also provide appropriate support for immigration laws and policies because immigration issues feed into mental health. Or an organization focused on family and community support among Asian Americans and Pacific Islanders can also focus on LGBTQ young people. The data we have gathered can informed services at organizations such as Desi Rainbow Parents & Allies, National Black Justice Coalition (NBJC), and the Ali Forney Center, among others.

Researchers must be intentional about which aspects of sexual orientation and gender identity are most relevant to the questions they are trying to answer when designing their studies. They must use survey items closely matched to those categories. Researchers must find a balance between nuance and analytic utility—allowing young people to describe their own identities in addition to using categorical descriptors. This can look like including open-ended questions or longer lists of identity options. Taking steps like these are critical for collecting and analyzing data that reflect the multitudes of this diverse group of young people. I urge researchers to apply an intersectional lens to their work and public health officials and youth-serving organizations to tailor services and programming to meet the unique needs of all young people. That's because a "one-size-fits-all" approach has never and will never work when the goal is to save lives.

If You Need Help

If you or someone you know is struggling or having thoughts of suicide, help is available. Call or text the 988 Suicide & Crisis Lifeline at 988 or use the online Lifeline Chat. LGBTQ+ Americans can reach out to the Trevor Project by texting START to 678-678 or calling 1-866-488-7386.

This is an opinion and analysis article, and the views expressed by the author or authors are not necessarily those of Scientific American.

About the Author

Myeshia Price (she/they) is director of research science at the Trevor Project, the leading suicide prevention organization for LGBTQ young people. Leading with an intersectional lens, Price oversees the development, analysis and translation of research findings to inform policies and practices that aim to end suicide among LGBTQ young people.

AI Chatbots Could Help Provide Therapy, but Caution Is Needed

By Sara Reardon

On Reddit forums, many users discussing mental health have enthused about their interactions with ChatGPT—OpenAI's artificial intelligence chatbot, which conducts humanlike conversations by predicting the likely next word in a sentence. "ChatGPT is better than my therapist," one user wrote, adding that the program listened and responded as the person talked about their struggles with managing their thoughts. "In a very scary way, I feel HEARD by ChatGPT." Other users have talked about asking ChatGPT to act as a therapist because they cannot afford a real one.

The excitement is understandable, particularly considering the shortage of mental health professionals in the U.S. and worldwide. People seeking psychological help often face long waiting lists, and insurance doesn't always cover therapy and other mental health care. Advanced chatbots such as ChatGPT and Google's Bard could help in administering therapy, even if they can't ultimately replace therapists. "There's no place in medicine that [chatbots] will be so effective as in mental health," says Thomas Insel, former director of the National Institute of Mental Health and co-founder of Vanna Health, a start-up company that connects people with serious mental illnesses to care providers. In the field of mental health, "we don't have procedures: we have chat; we have communication."

But many experts worry about whether tech companies will respect vulnerable users' privacy, program appropriate safeguards to ensure AIs don't provide incorrect or harmful information or prioritize treatment aimed toward affluent healthy people at the expense of people with severe mental illnesses. "I appreciate the algorithms have improved, but ultimately I don't think they are going to address the messier social realities that people are in when they're seeking help," says Julia Brown, an anthropologist at the University of California, San Francisco.

A Therapist's Assistant

The concept of "robot therapists" has been around since at least 1990, when computer programs began offering psychological interventions that walk users through scripted procedures such as cognitive-behavioral therapy. More recently, popular apps such as those offered by Woebot Health and Wysa have adopted more advanced AI algorithms that can converse with users about their concerns. Both companies say their apps have had more than a million downloads. And chatbots are already being used to screen patients by administering standard questionnaires. Many mental health providers at the U.K.'s National Health Service use a chatbot from a company called Limbic to diagnose certain mental illnesses.

New programs such as ChatGPT, however, are much better than previous AIs at interpreting the meaning of a human's question and responding in a realistic manner. Trained on immense amounts of text from across the Internet, these large language model (LLM) chatbots can adopt different personas, ask a user questions and draw accurate conclusions from the information the user gives them.

As an assistant for human providers, Insel says, LLM chatbots could greatly improve mental health services, particularly among marginalized, severely ill people. The dire shortage of mental health professionals—particularly those willing to work with imprisoned people and those experiencing homelessness—is exacerbated by the amount of time providers need to spend on paperwork, Insel says. Programs such as ChatGPT could easily summarize patients' sessions, write necessary reports, and allow therapists and psychiatrists to spend more time treating people. "We could enlarge our workforce by 40 percent by off-loading documentation and reporting to machines," he says.

But using ChatGPT as a therapist is a more complex matter. While some people may balk at the idea of spilling their secrets to a machine, LLMs can sometimes give better responses than many human users, says Tim Althoff, a computer scientist at the University of Washington. His group has studied how crisis counselors express empathy in text messages and trained LLM programs to give writers feedback based on strategies used by those who are the most effective at getting people out of crisis.

"There's a lot more [to therapy] than putting this into ChatGPT and seeing what happens," Althoff says. His group has been working with the nonprofit Mental Health America to develop a tool based on the algorithm that powers ChatGPT. Users type in their negative thoughts, and the program suggests ways they can reframe those specific thoughts into something positive. More than 50,000 people have used the tool so far, and Althoff says users are more than seven times more likely to complete the program than a similar one that gives canned responses.

Empathetic chatbots could also be helpful for peer support groups such as TalkLife and Koko, in which people without specialized training send other users helpful, uplifting messages. In a study published in *Nature Machine Intelligence* in January, when Althoff and his colleagues had peer supporters craft messages using an empathetic chatbot and found that nearly half the recipients preferred the texts written with the chatbot's help over those written solely by humans and rated them as 20 percent more empathetic.

But having a human in the loop is still important. In an experiment that Koko co-founder Rob Morris described on Twitter, the company's leaders found that users could often tell if responses came from a bot, and they disliked those responses once they knew the messages were AI-generated. (The experiment provoked a backlash online, but Morris says the app contained a note informing users that messages were partly written with AI.) It appears that "even though we're sacrificing efficiency and quality, we prefer the messiness of human interactions that existed before," Morris says.

Researchers and companies developing mental health chatbots insist that they are not trying to replace human therapists but rather to supplement them. After all, people can talk with a chatbot whenever they want, not just when they can get an appointment, says Woebot Health's chief program officer Joseph Gallagher. That can speed the therapy process, and people can come to trust the bot. The bond, or therapeutic alliance, between a therapist and a client is thought to account for a large percentage of therapy's effectiveness.

In a study of 36,000 users, researchers at Woebot Health, which does not use ChatGPT, found that users develop a trusting bond with the company's chatbot within four days, based on a standard questionnaire used to measure therapeutic alliance, as compared with weeks with a human therapist. "We hear from people, 'There's no way I could have told this to a human,'" Gallagher says. "It lessens the stakes and decreases vulnerability."

Risks of Outsourcing Care

But some experts worry the trust could backfire, especially if the chatbots aren't accurate. A theory called automation bias suggests that people are more likely to trust advice from a machine than from a human—even if it's wrong. "Even if it's beautiful nonsense, people tend more to accept it," says Evi-Anne van Dis, a clinical psychology researcher at Amsterdam UMC in the Netherlands.

And chatbots are still limited in the quality of advice they can give. They may not pick up on information that a human would clock as indicative of a problem, such as a severely underweight person asking how to lose weight. Van Dis is concerned that AI programs will be biased against certain groups of people if the medical literature they were trained on—likely from wealthy, western countries—contains biases. They may miss cultural differences in the way mental illness is expressed or draw wrong conclusions based on how a user writes in that person's second language.

The greatest concern is that chatbots could hurt users by suggesting that a person discontinue treatment, for instance, or even by advocating self-harm. In recent weeks the National Eating Disorders Association (NEDA) has come under fire for shutting down its helpline, previously staffed by humans, in favor of a chatbot called Tessa, which was not based on generative AI but instead gave scripted advice to users. According to social media posts by some users, Tessa sometimes gave weight-loss tips, which can be triggering to people with eating disorders. NEDA suspended the chatbot on May 30 and said in a statement that it is reviewing what happened.

"In their current form, they're not appropriate for clinical settings, where trust and accuracy are paramount," says Ross Harper, chief executive officer of Limbic, regarding AI chatbots that have not been adapted for medical purposes. He worries that mental health app developers who don't modify the underlying algorithms to include good scientific and medical practices will inadvertently develop something harmful. "It could set the whole field back," Harper says.

Chaitali Sinha, head of clinical development and research at Wysa, says that her industry is in a sort of limbo while governments figure out how to regulate AI programs like ChatGPT. "If you can't regulate it, you can't use it in clinical settings," she says. Van Dis adds that the public knows little about how tech companies collect and use the information users feed into chatbots—raising concerns about potential confidentiality violations—or about how the chatbots were trained in the first place.

Limbic, which is testing a ChatGPT-based therapy app, is trying to address this by adding a separate program that limits ChatGPT's responses to evidence-based therapy. Harper says that health regulators can evaluate and regulate this and similar "layer" programs as medical products, even if laws regarding the underlying AI program are still pending.

Wysa is currently applying to the U.S. Food and Drug Administration for its cognitive-behavioral-therapy-delivering chatbot to be approved as a medical device, which Sinha says could happen within a year. Wysa uses an AI that is not ChatGPT, but Sinha says the company may consider generative AIs once regulations become clearer.

Brown worries that without regulations in place, emotionally vulnerable users will be left to determine whether a chatbot is reliable, accurate, and helpful. She is also concerned that for-profit chatbots will be primarily developed for the "worried well"–people who can afford therapy and app subscriptions–rather than isolated individuals who might be most at risk but don't know how to seek help.

Ultimately, Insel says, the question is whether some therapy is better than none. "Therapy is best when there's a deep connection, but that's often not what happens for many people, and it's hard to get high-quality care," he says. It would be nearly impossible to train enough therapists to meet the demand, and partnerships between professionals and carefully developed chatbots could ease the burden immensely. "Getting an army of people empowered with these tools is the way out of this," Insel says.

About the Author

Sara Reardon is a freelance journalist based in Bozeman, Mont. She is a former staff reporter at Nature, New Scientist *and* Science *and has a master's degree in molecular biology.*

Electrical Brain Stimulation May Alleviate Obsessive-Compulsive Behaviors

By Diana Kwon

Obsessive-compulsive disorder (OCD) is marked by repetitive, anxiety-inducing thoughts, urges, and compulsions, such as excessive cleaning, counting, and checking. These behaviors are also prevalent in the general population: one study in a large sample of U.S. adults found more than a quarter had experienced obsessions or compulsions at some point in their life. Although most of these individuals do not develop full-blown OCD, such symptoms can still interfere with daily life. A new study, published on January 18 in *Nature Medicine,* hints that these behaviors may be alleviated by stimulating the brain with an electrical current—without the need to insert electrodes under the skull.

Robert Reinhart, a neuroscientist at Boston University, and his group drew on two parallel lines of research for this study. First, evidence suggests that obsessive-compulsive behaviors may arise as a result of overlearning habits—leading to their excessive repetition—and abnormalities in brain circuits involved in learning from rewards. Separately, studies point to the importance of high-frequency rhythms in the so-called high-beta/low-gamma range (also referred to as simply beta-gamma) in decision-making and learning from positive feedback.

Drawing on these prior observations, Shrey Grover, a doctoral student in Reinhart's lab, hypothesized with others in the team that manipulating beta-gamma rhythms in the orbitofrontal cortex (OFC)—a key region in the reward network located in the front of the brain—might disrupt the ability to repetitively pursue rewarding choices. In doing so, the researchers thought, the intervention could reduce obsessive-compulsive behaviors associated with maladaptive habits.

To test this hypothesis, Grover and his colleagues carried out a two-part study. The first segment was aimed at identifying whether the high-frequency brain activity influenced how well people were able to learn from rewards. The team recruited 60 volunteers and first used electroencephalography to pinpoint the unique frequencies of beta-gamma rhythms in the OFC that were active in a given individual while that person took part in a task that involved associating symbols with monetary wins or losses. Previous work had shown that applying stimulation based on the particular patterns of rhythms in a person's brain may enhance the effectiveness of the procedure.

The participants were then split into three groups, all of whom received a noninvasive form of brain stimulation known as transcranial alternating current stimulation (tACS), which was applied to the OFC for 30 minutes over five consecutive days. Each group had a different type of stimulation: One received personalized currents tuned to an individual's beta-gamma frequencies. Another was exposed to an "active" placebo, consisting of stimulations at a lower frequency. And the third was a "passive" placebo group in which no significant current was applied to the brain. Those who received the personalized beta-gamma stimulation became less able to make optimal choices on the reward-based learning tasks—changes not observed in the two placebo groups.

Further assessment of the participants' behavior using computational models of reward-based learning suggested that the personalized tACS disrupted the learning process by making people more likely to try out different options rather than sticking with only one—even if they were less likely to result in a reward.

These findings set the stage for the second part of the study, in which the team set out to examine whether manipulating the beta-gamma rhythms typically engaged during reward-based learning would influence obsessive-compulsive behaviors. The researchers carried out a similar set of experiments on another set of volunteers: 64 people who did not have a formal OCD diagnosis but who exhibited symptoms such as checking, hoarding, and obsessing.

Participants received either personalized beta-gamma stimulation or an active placebo. Those in the personalized beta-gamma group experienced a reduction in compulsive behaviors that persisted for up to three months. And those with more of those obsessive-compulsive characteristics prior to stimulation exhibited the biggest changes.

According to Grover, the team decided to study people with symptoms of OCD but no diagnosis of the disorder because researchers have increasingly been viewing obsessive-compulsive behaviors on a mild-to-severe spectrum. And even in the absence of clinically diagnosed OCD, such symptoms can cause significant distress. "By examining a nonclinical population exhibiting a range of obsessive-compulsive behaviors, we were able to examine the effectiveness of [an intervention] that may be helpful to a larger pool of individuals," Grover says. Yet the researchers' findings also suggest "that if we were to extend such an intervention to individuals diagnosed with obsessive-compulsive disorder or to other conditions of compulsivity—gambling disorder, addiction, some forms of eating disorders—we might be able to observe strong effects."

The long-lasting effects on obsessive-compulsive behaviors is "quite impressive," says Trevor Robbins, a professor of cognitive neuroscience at the University of Cambridge, who was not involved in this research. "[Neuromodulation] is certainly a treatment that should be investigated rigorously for conditions like OCD."

Carolyn Rodriguez, a psychiatrist and neuroscientist at Stanford University, who was also not involved in the study, says that because it was carried out in a nonclinical population without a formal diagnosis, the implications of these findings remain to be seen. "The neurobiology of people who are nonclinical but have these kinds of behaviors may be different than individuals who are diagnosed with OCD," she adds. "These findings are an interesting start, [but] we need to understand how it's relevant to people who have OCD." Rodriguez also points out that there are already several treatments available for the condition, including medication, therapy, and a Food and Drug Administration–approved device that utilizes transcranial magnetic stimulation (TMS), a noninvasive method that uses magnetic fields to stimulate the brain. (Rodriguez is currently leading a clinical trial of TMS for OCD.)

The potential therapeutic effects of tACS on memory, food craving, and other neural processes have been tested in dozens of studies in the past. Questions have been raised about whether this method actually exerts any meaningful changes in the brain, however. In the new study, what, exactly, the high-frequency tACS did to the brain remains unknown. But Grover notes that the researchers' two placebo conditions—particularly the one that involves stimulating at a different frequency—provide strong evidence that the high-frequency stimulation was responsible for the behavioral effects the team observed.

Grover and his colleagues are currently working on further experiments to pinpoint the mechanisms underlying their intervention. And they hope to conduct studies with clinical populations diagnosed with OCD in the near future. "[The recent paper] is just a preliminary step toward further understanding why this high-frequency activity is so important for obsessive-compulsive behavior," Grover says. "The fact that we can observe changes in these symptoms even now suggests there may actually be clinical benefit to this—and gives us all the more reason to try to extend the findings of this research."

About the Author

Diana Kwon is a freelance journalist who covers health and the life sciences. She is based in Berlin.

Brain Scans May Predict Optimal Mental Health Treatments

By John Gabrieli

Every day people with common mental health difficulties receive prescriptions for therapies that will not help them. Finding treatments that work for these patients entails an arduous process of trial and error. Each failed therapy risks leaving a patient despondent about whether anything will ever help.

Depression illustrates poignantly what can go wrong. By most measures, half to two thirds of patients diagnosed with depression will fail to benefit from any particular treatment. Research protocols for depression consist of clinical trials that typically evaluate the general effectiveness of a drug or behavioral therapy based on the average benefit for a patient. They overlook, however, the wide range of individual patient outcomes, ranging from full recovery to no benefit at all. The largest and longest evaluation of drug treatment for depression, a National Institutes of Health study of thousands of patients at multiple U.S. health care institutions called STAR*D, illustrates what can happen. Every patient in the study received an initial drug, and about a third showed major improvements. Only about a quarter of those who failed to respond to the first drug benefited from the second. After a third and fourth prescription for other drugs, 70 percent of patients demonstrated substantial progress. But most had to experience one or more treatment failures before finding a drug that worked.

Failed treatments not only prolong distress, they also discourage patients from seeking help. Participants in STAR*D knew they had possible access to other treatments in the next phase of the study, but even so many gave up. A substantial number of patients dropped out of the study after an initial failed pharmaceutical treatment, about 30 percent after a second therapy and about 42 percent following a third. (Behavioral treatment of depression using the form of talk therapy known as cognitive-behavioral therapy, or CBT, also yields a strong benefit for about half of patients.)

Explanations for the difficulties psychiatrists face relate to the imprecisions and economic imperatives of drug development. Two people diagnosed with the same mental health disorder can respond in wholly different ways to the same drug treatment because of the current inability to assess who will respond to which treatment. Yet pharmaceutical companies typically aim for the largest possible market rather than tailoring treatment to smaller patient groups that exhibit a specific form of depression or another psychiatric disorder. Drug developers also lack the tools to implement a more precise approach. Diagnostic techniques to predict whether a person will profit from a given treatment are not part of routine medical practice.

In recent years various brain-imaging techniques, combined with sophisticated algorithms that analyze neural activity, have started to reveal brain differences among people that predict whether a given drug or talk therapy will lift a patient out of a depression or relieve severe social anxiety. Early versions of these diagnostic techniques have also shown promise in determining whether an alcoholic might relapse—and they have even begun to identify whether a student will face educational difficulties in reading and mathematics.

Brain scans to tailor treatments embody a new form of personalized medicine, an approach that often relies on customizing therapies based on an individual's genetics. Undoubtedly, genes can predispose a person to mental illness. For any one individual, though, only a weak relation exists between a given gene and common psychiatric disorders. Experience also plays a pivotal role in determining which genes become activated in the brain. Although imaging has many limitations, it approximates what is happening in the brain through the combination of genes and experience. At the moment, it can forecast the prospects for a treatment with greater precision than genetics alone. As these techniques are refined, however, the melding of brain and genetic measures may one day offer still more accurate predictions.

Will It Work?

A study that my group at the Massachusetts Institute of Technology performed in collaboration with clinician-scientists at Boston University and Massachusetts General Hospital demonstrates the prospects for predicting whether a treatment might work. Together we studied how patients with social anxiety disorder responded to CBT. Social anxiety, characterized by an intense fear of interacting with others, remains one of the most common psychiatric conditions in the U.S. Its severe form is often so disabling that the affected person cannot hold a job. In our study, all patients received behavioral therapy. We wanted to find out whether brain measurements taken *before treatment* could predict who would benefit substantially from CBT.

Patients viewed faces with either neutral or negative (angry) emotional expressions while we recorded responses using functional magnetic resonance imaging (fMRI), a type of scan that measures changes in brain blood flow. We also asked a series of questions to quantify the severity of their anxieties. Patients with greater responses to angry faces in regions at the back of the brain, which processes faces and other visual objects, were more likely to benefit from CBT. Using such a brain measure more than tripled the accuracy of predicting which individuals would benefit from CBT compared with results from a conventional severity rating derived from questionnaires.

Another approach we used to assess the effectiveness of CBT combined two techniques. One, known as diffusion tensor imaging, evaluates how well connections established by fiber tracts, or white matter, enable different brain regions to communicate with one another. White matter consists of bundles of long, protruding extensions from neurons called axons that are covered in a whitish, fatty material known as myelin.

The second technique gauges what brain connections link together when a person lies at rest inside the MRI machine. With these data, researchers concocted a map of brain networks. From it, the team created a diagnostic measure, a biomarker, that produced a fivefold improvement in predicting which patients would benefit from CBT. Other studies, such as those by Greg Siegle of the University of Pittsburgh, have confirmed that a similar strategy seems effective in determining how patients with depression respond to CBT.

Predicting the response to a drug for a psychiatric disorder can combine imaging with more conventional types of psychological tests. Andrea N. Goldstein-Piekarski of Stanford University and her colleagues examined responses to antidepressant medications. They interviewed patients about early life stress and then used fMRI to assess activity in the amygdala, a brain structure that processes emotions. In the scanner, patients looked at images of a series of happy facial expressions. Combining information about a person's early life stress and his or her amygdala's responses to faces hinted at whether that individual would benefit from antidepressant medications. The Siegle and Goldstein-Piekarski studies did not compare talk therapy with medication. But Helen Mayberg of Emory University has shown that brain imaging can also reveal whether an individual with depression is more likely to be helped by talk therapy versus a medication.

Predicting Relapse

Treatments for alcoholism, drug addiction, smoking, and obesity share the aim of having users abstain or pare back their use of drugs, tobacco or food. Here, too, imaging techniques may play a role in predicting who will relapse into addictive habits. Half of patients treated for alcohol abuse go back to drinking within a year of treatment, and similar reversion rates occur for stimulants such as cocaine.

There is little scientific evidence for determining the length and duration of programs such as a 28-day in-patient rehabilitation at a treatment facility. Research has yet to show whether a shorter or longer course of therapy would prove more effective. Ideally, studies could ascertain if a given patient will relapse in six months or a year, allowing program length to be tailored to an individual's needs.

Imaging studies that make predictions of the outcome for alcohol and drug dependency and obesity are not as common as those looking at depression. Still, a number suggest that brain measures might foresee who will succeed in abstaining after treatment has ended. A study at the University of California, San Diego, found that brain imaging performed at the end of treatment for methamphetamine abuse predicted which patients would relapse during the following 12 months.

In an obesity-prevention study using MRI imaging at the University of Alabama, investigators discovered that reward areas of the brain that direct attention to food—the nucleus accumbens, the anterior cingulate, and the insula—became active in a group of 25 obese and overweight individuals who looked at images of high-calorie fare before entering a 12-week weight-loss counseling program. Greater activation in these areas predicted who would have the most difficulty in shedding pounds once the program was over. Participants who went into the scanner afterward and who showed high activation of the insula and other attention and reward processing areas had more difficulty in sticking with the regimen nine months later.

Brain imaging may even help formulate the types of messages that health professionals use to encourage patients to adopt healthy behaviors. Emily Falk, then at the University of California, Los Angeles, and her colleagues asked those in their study to learn the proper technique for using sunscreen to prevent sunburn and skin cancers. Researchers recorded fMRI responses as participants watched slides that prescribed preventive measures. Participants then described their attitudes toward sunscreen use and their intentions to use it after receiving a supply of sun-protective towelettes. A week later the group received e-mails asking whether they had actually applied the lotion. Individuals who had logged greater activity during the viewing session in one brain area, the medial prefrontal cortex, which regulates beliefs and a sense of self, ended up using more sunscreen. Brain scans provided an objective measure of the program's effectiveness, extending beyond an individual's subjective evaluation of whether the health information helped.

Observation of brain activity may also assist in discovering the best approach to dissuade people from continuing to smoke. A 2010 paper in *Biological Psychiatry* from Harvard Medical School found that among 21 women, a high response to smoking-related pictures in two brain regions—the insula and the dorsal anterior cingulate cortex—forecast an inability to quit.

Better Learners

Children's education might benefit as well from brain imaging to predict difficulties in learning to read (dyslexia) or do math (dyscalculia). Teachers and parents try to help, but education operates largely on the model of waiting to fail. Students receive some guidance from teachers until they reach a point when they become discouraged, and then learning tends to break down.

What if instructional support did not merely react to failures but could anticipate specific forms of teaching that could be adapted to the needs of individual students? Some recent findings indicate that brain imaging can help predict students' future performance. Brain assessments, in fact, can sometimes outperform conventional educational and psychological measures at foreseeing how well a student will do in the classroom.

Among children with dyslexia, individuals vary greatly in their ability to compensate for reading difficulties by devising their own strategies that let them catch up to their classmates. Fumiko Hoeft, now at the University of California, San Francisco, and I measured brain fMRI responses to printed words in children with dyslexia around 14 years of age who also received extensive psychological testing. Then we examined the same children again 30 months later to see how much they might have improved in reading. About half the children exhibited substantial gains.

None of the standard educational testing measures correlated with future reading progress, but the brain scans combined with an analytical technique could make such predictions. Pattern-classification analysis, which delves into the complex data from fMRI brain scans using "big data" machine-learning algorithms, yielded more than 90 percent accuracy in characterizing whether a dyslexic child's reading would improve or continue to flounder two years after the images were captured. Other researchers have reported that electrical responses on the scalp (evoked response potentials) in young, preliterate children also predicted reading skills. Knowing what lies ahead may allow interventions prior to encountering reading difficulties, a strategy that spares children the sense of failure evoked by early struggles.

Math teaching may also profit. A study conducted by Vinod Menon of Stanford found that brain anatomy could identify whether a third-grade student had more of a chance of benefiting from a math-tutoring program that encouraged students to shift from counting to arithmetic fact retrieval (memorizing 2 + 3 = 5, for instance) as a basis for arithmetic problem solving. Conventional behavioral tests of math abilities or IQ failed to predict which student would not be helped by the program, but brain measures succeeded. In particular, the size of the right hippocampus, an area associated with memory, correlated with how much a student would progress.

These studies hold promise of laying the basis for a neuroscience-based methodology of personalized learning. If this research can eventually identify the best instructional approach for a student, educators could avoid the failures that occur later in childhood or adolescence when learning difficulties become more difficult to correct.

Wanted: Better Predictions

If brain measures show such promise for predicting whether an individual will respond to a mental health treatment or schooling, why are these methods not already in use? Several challenges linger before these techniques enter clinics and schools. First, the predictions need additional statistical rigor. In the studies so far, models have linked brain activity to already known outcomes, such as how much an individual benefited from a treatment. In that sense, they might be called postdiction rather than prediction. New studies must now ascertain whether these findings routinely make accurate forecasts.

For the prediction sciences to move forward in mental health and education, the research community must begin to design studies that compare results for two independent groups. A mathematical model from one group can be tested on the other to validate the model.

One intriguing approach known as leave-one-out cross-validation excludes an individual from the overall evaluation of the results of the group under analysis. Researchers create a model from other individuals in the study to predict a particular health or educational outcome. The model then goes on to forecast a result for the left-out individual. The entire process repeats for each study participant with the goal of creating a model that better guides selection of each new patient's treatment. Only a handful of studies have achieved such a high standard to date, but this level of rigor must be met for the practical use of brain imaging as a prediction technique.

Another barrier relates to the cost and availability of MRI brain imaging. Any economic calculation must balance the price for the procedure, which is often about $500 to $1,000 per hour, against the prospect of having to pay for physician and hospital visits, lost work productivity, and special education resources to support students falling behind. In some cases, other technologies might substitute for MRI, even while borrowing knowledge gleaned from the more expensive technique. Electroencephalography, which measures the brain's electrical activity, might, for instance, be adapted to take the place of MRI in some types of testing.

The promise and potential controversy surrounding MRI for clinical use show up in two recent studies. One by Joseph Piven of the University of North Carolina at Chapel Hill used fMRI to image 59 infants who were six months old to detect a heightened risk for autism spectrum disorder (ASD). The defining social and communication difficulties of autism rarely emerge at birth but typically only, with careful evaluation, at two years of age. Imaging studies of brain network activity at six months predicted correctly nine of the 11 infants who would be diagnosed with ASD some 18 months later. And the measurements also established that the other 48 would not be so classified. This kind of prediction could one day both calm the worries of parents whose infants will not progress to ASD and assist in devising early interventions to aid children at high risk.

Another prediction study attempted to build on evidence that impulsivity appears as a major risk factor for recidivism. A measure of brain activity for self-control could potentially help address the limited accuracy of expert advice in making decisions about bail, sentencing, and parole. Kent Kiehl, a professor of psychology, neuroscience, and law at the University of New Mexico, examined brain activity during an impulse-control task in 96 male offenders before their release from prison and then followed these men over a period of several years. The offenders performed a task during brain imaging intended to make impulse control difficult. They had to press a button as the character "X" appeared repeatedly on a computer screen. At the same time, they had to resist the temptation to press the button in the rare instances that the letter "K" appeared, thereby creating two conflicting impulses, depending on what was displayed on the screen.

The lab task helped to predict what happened to the men after their release from prison. The likelihood that a former inmate would face another arrest over a four-year period doubled if the offender had diminished activity in the anterior cingulate cortex, a brain region involved with cognitive control and resolving conflicting impulses. Brain scanning helped to better forecast future rearrest than conventional measures alone, such as scores on a psychopathy checklist, age, or lifetime substance abuse. An unpublished reanalysis of the data by Russ Poldrack, now at Stanford, suggests that the strength of this prediction lessens considerably when applying these results to prison populations other than the one surveyed (a suggestion partially countered by Kiehl and his colleagues).

All these studies raise a set of critical issues. How accurate should a prediction be to improve mental health treatments and educational practices? As a corollary, how can predictions made from brain scans help people rather than curtail their educational or employment opportunities? If we could better project future mental health or learning difficulties or even criminal activities, how would we, as a society, ensure that such predictions do not justify punitive policies and instead promote individual well-being? Ironically, the better prediction becomes over time, the more pressing the need emerges for an ethical framework to use such knowledge wisely.

References

"Dyslexia: A New Synergy between Education and Cognitive Neuroscience." John D. E. Gabrieli in *Science*, Vol. 325, pages 280–283; July 17, 2009.

"Toward Clinically Useful Neuroimaging in Depression Treatment: Prognostic Utility of Subgenual Cingulate Activity for Determining Depression Outcome in Cognitive Therapy across Studies, Scanners, and Patient Characteristics." Greg J. Siegle et al. in *Archives of General Psychiatry*, Vol. 69, No. 9, pages 913–924; September 2012.

"Prediction as a Humanitarian and Pragmatic Contribution from Human Cognitive Neuroscience." John D. E. Gabrieli et al. in *Neuron*, Vol. 85, No. 1, pages 11–26; January 7, 2015.

About the Author

John Gabrieli is director of the Athinoula A. Martinos Imaging Center at the McGovern Institute for Brain Research at the Massachusetts Institute of Technology. He also holds the Grover Hermann Professorship at the Harvard-M.I.T. Program of Health Sciences and Technology.

Science Shows How to Protect Kids' Mental Health, but It's Being Ignored

By Mitch Prinstein and Kathleen A. Ethier

Young people in the U.S. are experiencing a mental health crisis. Reports from the surgeon general, the American Academy of Pediatrics, and the American Psychological Association highlight the catastrophe, with families and children trying to get a moment with overwhelmed counselors, psychologists, or social workers.

Is this crisis caused by the pandemic? No. Those of us monitoring the health and well-being of youth know this storm began years ago. In 2022 we continue to fund a children's mental health system based on the needs of adult war veterans.

Scientific advances have identified effective school-based mental health practices, such as emotional-regulation training that teaches children how to cope with strong feelings, or screenings to detect mental health crises before they occur. These insights and practices have largely been ignored. Now is the time to act on them. Long-disproved theories of physical and mental health as being two independent systems have motivated the annual investment of billions in medical research and physician training, but staggeringly few resources are available to advance psychological science or a mental health workforce.

The need is clear. Data from the Centers for Disease Control and Prevention, where one of us (Ethier) is director of adolescent and school health, reveal that in 2009–2019, a remarkably high number of young people reported feeling severe emotional distress. Specifically, in 2019, 37 percent of high school students surveyed felt so sad and hopeless they couldn't participate in regular activities, about one in five seriously considered suicide, and about one in 11 attempted suicide. Adolescent girls and youth who identified as lesbian, gay, bisexual, or transgender or who were questioning their identity were overrepresented among those who considered or attempted suicide.

The CDC's Adolescent Behaviors and Experiences Survey, the first nationally representative survey of U.S. high school students during the pandemic, revealed that young people's lives were extremely disrupted. Almost a quarter of U.S. youth told us they experienced hunger; more than half had been emotionally abused by an adult in their homes. More than 60 percent of Asian students and more than half of Black students encountered racism. Emotional distress and suicidal thoughts and behaviors continued to worsen and were more significant among female and LGBTQ students.

The way forward can be found in science-based psychosocial approaches that one of us (Prinstein) and our psychologist colleagues have developed over recent decades. We have identified effective methods to prevent emotional or behavioral distress by teaching children skills to cope with stressors, develop healthy social relationships, and spot depression warning signs. For instance, during the pandemic, students who felt connected to others in school were less likely to experience indicators of poor mental health, as well as suicide plans and attempts.

Before the pandemic, by 2018, 79 percent of high schools identified safe spaces for LGBTQ youth, 96 percent had antiharassment policies, and 77 percent had inclusivity professional development for staff. Many schools also had inclusive, student-led clubs. Recent CDC research found that having such policies and practices improved mental health not only for LGBTQ students but for all young people. Similar results from antiracism programs make schools less toxic for historically marginalized youth and improve the health and well-being of all students.

These approaches are not controversial. Methods to increase connectedness include classroom-management techniques that reinforce attentive, cooperative, and collaborative behaviors, reduce peer victimization, and help youth understand how others feel and behave. Psychological prevention strategies can teach youth how to less frequently blame themselves for harsh experiences, help peers feel valued and included, and consider adaptive and healthy responses, even when confronted with aggression.

These programs require a commitment to the science of behavior and the deployment of innovative initiatives. And they need resources—to deploy these prevention approaches at scale and among populations most at need. Failure to address this mental health crisis will result in not only the distress of millions of U.S. youth today but a change in the productivity, success, and wellness of U.S. citizens at large as this generation matures.

About the Authors

Mitch Prinstein is chief science officer of the American Psychological Association. He holds a Ph.D. in clinical psychology from the University of Miami. Follow Prinstein on X (formerly Twitter) @mitchprinstein.

Kathleen A. Ethier is director of adolescent and school health at the Centers for Disease Control and Prevention. She holds a Ph.D. in social psychology from the City University of New York. Follow the CDC's Division of Adolescent and School Health on X (formerly Twitter) @CDC_DASH and follow Ethier on X (formerly Twitter) @ethierka. The findings and conclusions in this paper are those of the author and do not necessarily represent the official position of the Centers for Disease Control and Prevention.

GLOSSARY

algorithm A procedure or set of rules for solving a problem or performing a task, often applied to computer science and mathematics.

biomarker A measurable, objective indication of a medical state within a patient that serves as a sign of normal processes, abnormal processes, diseases, or other conditions.

causal Relating to the cause of something, giving rise to an action or condition.

cognitive Relating to or involved with the processes of thinking, perceiving, knowing, and reasoning.

dissociation A mental process that involves a break in how the mind processes information, such as memories, feelings, thoughts, and identity.

fatigue A feeling of extreme or constant tiredness and lack of energy, which can be physical, mental, or a combination of both.

insomnia A sleep disorder that makes it difficult to fall asleep or stay asleep.

intervention An action taken to improve a situation, especially a medical or psychiatric condition.

neurological Relating to diseases and conditions of the nervous system, including the brain.

unipolar Relating to a mental health condition that causes either depression or manic behavior, but not both.

variant Something that is different in some way from similar things or the standard version of that type of thing.

FURTHER INFORMATION

"The Hurt of Loneliness and Social Isolation," *Nature Mental Health*, March 11, 2024, https://www.nature.com/articles/s44220-024-00221-5.

"What Is Mental Health?," Substance Abuse and Mental Health Services Administration (SAMHSA), April 24, 2023, https://www.samhsa.gov/mental-health.

"Youth Risk Behavior Data Summary and Trends Report, 2011-2021," Centers for Disease Control and Prevention (CDC), February 13, 2023, https://www.cdc.gov/healthyyouth/data/yrbs/pdf/YRBS_Data-Summary-Trends_Report2023_508.pdf.

Booth, Robert. "'Social Media Is Like Driving with No Speed Limits': The US Surgeon General Fighting for Youngsters' Happiness," *The Guardian*, March 19, 2024, https://www.theguardian.com/media/2024/mar/20/vivek-murthy-us-surgeon-general-social-media-youth-happiness.

Farb, Norman, and Zindel Segal. "Paying Attention to Sensations Can Help Reset the Mind," *Scientific American*, March 8, 2024, https://www.scientificamerican.com/article/paying-attention-to-sensations-can-help-reset-the-mind/.

Miller, Jennifer. "When the Biggest Student Mental Health Advocates Are the Students," *The New York Times*, February 6, 2024, https://www.nytimes.com/2024/02/06/health/adolescents-mental-health-clubs.html.

Reuterskiold, Carl. "Global Mental Health: Can Technology Reduce the Stigma?," *Forbes*, September 27, 2023, https://www.forbes.com/sites/forbestechcouncil/2023/09/27/global-mental-health-can-technology-reduce-the-stigma/?sh=741f86476758

Saunders, Heather, and Rhiannon Euhus. "A Look at Substance Use and Mental Health Treatment Facilities Across the U.S.," KFF, February 2, 2024, https://www.kff.org/mental-health/issue-brief/a-look-at-substance-use-and-mental-health-treatment-facilities-across-the-u-s/.

CITATIONS

1.1 Is Too Little Play Hurting Our Kids? by Joseph Polidoro (December 4, 2023); 1.2 Treating Mental Health as Part of Climate Disaster Recovery by Anna Mattson (October 17, 2023); 1.3 'AI Anxiety' Is on the Rise—Here's How to Manage It by Lauren Leffer (October 2, 2023); 1.4 Why Just One Sleepless Night Makes People Emotionally Fragile by Eti Ben Simon (August 15, 2023); 1.5 How Much Worry about Mass Shootings Is Too Much? by Stephanie Pappas (June 4, 2023); 1.6 Social Media Can Harm Kids. Could New Regulations Help? by Jesse Greenspan (May 26, 2023); 1.7 COVID Can Cause Forgetfulness, Psychosis, Mania or a Stutter by Stephani Sutherland (January 21, 2021); 1.8 Climate Anxiety and Mental Illness by Brian Barnett and Amit Anand (October 10, 2020); 2.1 Aggression Disorders Are Serious, Stigmatized and Treatable by Abigail Marsh (February 9, 2024); 2.2 Mania May Be a Mental Illness in Its Own Right by Simon Makin (March 1, 2019); 2.3 Susceptibility to Mental Illness May Have Helped Humans Adapt over the Millennia by Dana G. Smith (March 1, 2019); 2.4 Analysis of a Million-Plus Genomes Points to Blurring Lines among Brain Disorders by Emily Willingham (June 22, 2018); 2.5 Mental Illness Is Far More Common Than We Knew by Aaron Reuben and Jonathan Schaefer (July 14, 2017); 2.6 Getting to the Root of the Problem: Stem Cells Are Revealing New Secrets about Mental Illness by Dina Fine Maron (February 27, 2018); 2.7 A New Way to Think about Mental Illness by Kristopher Nielsen (November 11, 2019); 3.1 Suppressing an Onrush of Toxic Thoughts Might Improve Your Mental Health by Ingrid Wickelgren (September 20, 2023); 3.2 Why Social Media Makes People Unhappy—And Simple Ways to Fix It by Daisy Yuhas (June 20, 2022); 3.3 How Long Does It Really Take to Form a Habit? by Jocelyn Solis-Moreira (January 24, 2024); 3.4 The Nature Cure by Jason G. Goldman (September 12, 2018); 3.5 The Way to Well-Being by Andrea Gawrylewski (February 13, 2018); 3.6 You Can't Fix Burnout With Self-Care by Shayla Love and Timmy Broderick (February 12, 2024); 4.1 Funding for Research on Psychedelics Is on the Rise, Along with Scientists' Hopes for Using Them by Rachel Nuwer (November 10, 2023); 4.2 A Newly Discovered Brain Signal Marks Recovery from Depression by Ingrid Wickelgren (September 20, 2023); 4.3 To Solve the LGBTQ Youth Mental Health Crisis, Our Research Must Be More Nuanced by Myeshia Price (July 25, 2023); 4.4 AI Chatbots Could Help Provide Therapy, but Caution Is Needed by Sara Reardon (June 14, 2023); 4.5 Electrical Brain Stimulation May Alleviate Obsessive-Compulsive Behaviors by Diana Kwon (January 19, 2021); 4.6 Brain Scans May Predict Optimal Mental Health Treatments by John Gabrieli (March 1, 2018); 4.7 Science Shows How to Protect Kids' Mental Health, but It's Being Ignored by Mitch Prinstein and Kathleen A. Ethier (May 31, 2022).

Each author biography was accurate at the time the article was originally published.

INDEX

O

obsessive-compulsive disorder
(OCD), 47, 75–77, 88,
139–142

P

play, 8–12, 15
post-traumatic stress disorder
(PTSD), 16–18, 27, 76, 92,
94–96, 118
psychedelics, 117–122
psychopathy, 52, 56, 151

S

schizophrenia, 44, 53, 59, 70,
72–73, 75–77, 81, 84,
86–88
shootings, 12, 16, 31–33
social media, 11–14, 34–39, 45,
97–101
suicide and suicidal behavior,
8, 27, 34, 38–39, 49, 64,
129–132, 153–154